THE ZOMBIE EFFECT

ROGER SAMPSON

SEVERED PRESS

HOBART TASMANIA

THE ZOMBIE EFFECT

"There will one day spring from the brain of science a machine of force so fearful in its potentialities, so absolutely terrifying, that even man, the fighter, who will dare torture and death in order to inflict torture and death, will be appalled, and so abandon war forever."

Thomas A Edison

CHAPTER 1

Jackson Hart was always one of the smartest people in the room. From the age of four, when he tested off the charts and was an absolute book worm, his parents knew he would be something special. In spite of his name, which when spoken aloud sounds more like a ROM-COM character than a brainiac, Jack never paid attention to the insults thrown his way. He was too busy out studying everyone else. And he was good at it. No, he was a master. Though with all that brain power, Jack never knew he would need every inch of grey matter in order to save the world. If that was even possible.

Being smarter than everyone else does have its drawbacks. Conversations are often boring. Interactions with other people often banal. In addition to all of that, they have a tendency to be socially awkward. Jack was never suave in his flirtations, but he wasn't exactly a social leper. His main challenge was avoiding talking over a fair haired maiden's head. Being book smart doesn't translate well to understanding the female personality. Boredom is a dangerous thing, especially for someone like Jack. Idle hands and all. So Jack developed another social activity. One worthy of his intellect. Juvenile delinquency.

There is a great rush of adrenaline when intellect is applied outside the scope of the rules. Jack learned this for the first time at age eight, when he hacked into his school's server and gave all of his classmates A's in every class, without leaving a trace of his being there. Not being caught became the game. The thrill of the hunt. So when it came to attending Dr. Cliff Barrister's lecture at the Barrister Institute, Jack decided his entrance was just as important as his presence.

Jack and his classmate Barry, a portly young man who fancies himself a bit of an adrenaline junkie himself, sneak very Ethan Hunt-esque along the wall leading to the loading dock at the rear of the Barrister Institute. Barry had received some "intel" during his latest online gaming binge, where his avatar looks more like James Bond than his real self, which was guaranteed to give them forbidden entrance next to the dumpster. Barry trips over his own shoe. Jack glares at him. Barry shrugs. The pair finally reach the red illuminated lock. Jack reaches into his bag and retrieves the piece of paper with the code. He enters the code. Nothing happens. He enters it a second time. Same nonreaction. Jack glares at Barry. "He told me it was good," Barry retorts. Jack sighs to himself and glares at Barry. He reaches into his backpack and retrieves his self designed code breaker tool. The contraption resembles an old fashioned garage door opener with red and blue wires sticking out of the top. He pops the face plate off the lock and attaches the leads. He flicks the switch on the front of the box and the scrolling numbers stop one by one until the light changes from red to green and the lock clicks open. Jack smiles, disconnects the electrodes and slithers through the doorway. Barry clumsily attempts to replace the faceplate and it clangs to the ground. Jack glares at Barry again with bulging eyes. "Sorry," Barry squeaks.

The interior of the loading area and adjacent hallway are barren white, as if designed to feel sterile and creepy simultaneously. The lack of light after hours gives life to imaginations of ghosts and goblins creeping in every shadow. Jack navigates the halls with ease as Barry struggles to keep up, convinced that one misstep will lead to his being taken to a dark end by monsters. Finally the pair see light ahead and Barry breathes a sigh of relief. Jack chuckles to himself. Hard to imagine how Barry has lived this long, Jack thinks to himself.

They emerge to the main foyer of the institute. From the main entrance to the entrance of the auditorium is a two story foyer with hanging incandescent lights. The room has been outfitted with a bar, several food stations with standing room tables. Several hundred guests line the room dressed as if attending a gala. Gowns flow freely and tuxedos choke the necks of the high society donors of all types as members of the staff of the institute work the room. The Barrister Institute excels in biological and chemical studies, including the search for the cures for a variety of diseases, the study of biological anomalies and even weapons development, not that the latter is widely known. The institute used to rely almost exclusively on government contracts, but with the last three administrations funneling money out of the research sector into other areas, private funding has become their life blood. So many palms to press and drinks to buy. Until you try it, you have no idea how tough it is to separate the affluent from their money or influence. But Dr. Cliff Barrister has become quite adept at it. More from necessity than talent.

As Jack takes a step into the room the pair are immediately met by Parker. Parker is the head of security at the Barrister Institute. A 40-something former Police captain, he keeps a tight ship. Little does Jack know that Parker's security system immediately notified him when the faceplate was removed from the security lock in the loading dock. Or maybe Jack knew and didn't care. In either event, here they were together.

"May I help you gentlemen?" Parker politely asks. Barry takes a step back as Jack smirks.

"Here for Dr. Barrister's lecture," Jack responds. Parker looks over Jack's appearance. Unimpressed by Jack's Hawaiian shirt, cargo shorts and sandals, Parker shakes his head no. "Invitation only." Jack retrieves an envelope from his backpack and hands it to Parker. Parker smiles and opens the invitation. "Where's his?" Parker asks.

"Plus one, Parker," Jack smiles. This is clearly not the first time these two have danced.In the mundane world of facility security, Parker enjoys the game.

"Aren't you a little under dressed?" Parker asks with a grin. Jack looks himself over. Very pleased with himself, he raises his arms and shrugs his shoulders. Parker stares at Jack for a long beat and hands him back the invitation. "You trying to piss him off?" Parker inquires like Captain Obvious. Jack winks and smiles.

"Never," he says. Parker steps aside as Jack and Barry stroll past. Parker shakes his head and chuckles.

Jack plucks a champagne glass from a server's tray as they make their way through the reception area. Several heads glance awkwardly in their direction. They approach the entrance to the auditorium where a poster rests on an easel that reads "Earth's Natural Defenses, Are Humans Really The Top Of The Food Chain? By Dr. Cliff Barrister". The pair enter the auditorium.

The Barrister Institute auditorium is laid out like a small theater. It contains three sections of seats fifteen rows deep with ten seats in each of the front rows and twenty five seats in the back row of the middle section. Red velvet curtains line the exterior walls and the back of the stage. Incandescent lamps pour light in the aisles and stage. Ushers greet and lead guests to their seats. Jack and Barry plod along with an usher to the left side section back row. Jack plops down in his seat. He surveys the room and chuckles lightly to himself, amused at the decadence on display. What would a research institute need with a theater fit for movies anyway? The ridiculous nature of fund raising, if it does nothing else, brings into the light the narcissism that hides in plain sight.

As if to announce the show about to begin, the lights flicker on and off. Jack feels a momentary sense of pride of interning in a place so overtly affluent, in spite of his humble beginnings. Being smarter than the bulk of the brain trust in the room can make humility a challenge. The irony is not lost on Jack.

Cliff Barrister is a polished professional in his 50s.His long tenured research facility has been home to many a discovery over the years. Then again, it's been some time since they've enjoyed a significant find or success, instead finding a way to stretch the financial and influential benefits of past successes as far as possible, just like Cliff himself. To say he's desperate for a breakthrough would be extreme, unless you could see behind the façade he presents to the world through his tightly pressed tuxedo. Like any successful businessman, he presents himself in a positive way and hides his fears behind layers of diplomas. But his need for a breakthrough is great. His breakthrough is on the way, just not in the way he thinks. He takes the stage to a standing ovation. The curtain behind him parts gracefully to reveal the Barrister Institute logo and title for the evening's lecture. Cliff attaches his lapel microphone and addresses the gathering.

"In my twenty years in the field of Microbiology and Life Science, one truth has always held true. The belief that man rules the earth is arrogance and ignorance. Man is but a guest here. And yet he continues to abuse the very home he was tasked to steward. The earth was here before man, and will be here long after man is gone. We would be wise to be cautious. Earth is capable of defending herself. She's done it before, and she'll do it again. Just ask the dinosaurs." Cliff narrates.

Cliff began his career an ideological scientist whose dream was to change the world. In fact, Cliff and Rachel began their lives together by having some remarkable breakthroughs. Breakthroughs that gave birth to the Barrister Institute. But as history can attest, success and fame are like firecrackers. They burn hot and bright but are over in a moment. For Cliff, that moment has lasted almost twenty years. The clock is ticking on his legacy. His past success is quite adequate for an ordinary man's legacy. But Cliff is anything but ordinary. True greatness requires front page news on a regular, consistent basis. Cliff is long overdue. If that weren't motivation enough, the funding for the Barrister Institute comes primarily from private sources. It was once government funded, but years without breakthrough dried up those wells. That forced Cliff to seek funding elsewhere. He found it, but at great price. Some of it from private affluent individuals who benefited financially from Cliff's past success. The rest from a single corporate donor. But the pressure for success is mounting, and nobody feels it more than Cliff. He needs a breakthrough soon. His wait is almost over.

The reception hall overflows with guests of all types. Friends, colleagues and even competitors suffering from morbid curiosity line the hall, consuming food and drink as if it were the last supper. Palm pressing and politically correct banter win the day in the hopes that much needed capital will once again fill the coffers of the Barrister Institute. What once was a science facility in its purest sense has devolved into an organizational survivalist strategy. Jack and Barry stand at the back of the hall, overseeing the games. Jack smiles as he chugs the champagne glass dangling from his fingertips. Barry looks like he's lost, wondering how he ever got here. He's in over his head and he knows it and would love nothing more than to melt back into the wall behind him. Jack spies Cliff a short distance away performing his host duties to perfection.

"Thank you, Bob. Your support means a lot to the institute. Always has," Cliff encourages. Cliff spies Logan Gibson from Hicks Corporation heading in his direction. Cliff despises Logan.Or more to the point, he despises what Hicks represents to his dream. If changing the world for the better was the plan, Hicks is the antithesis. But without Hicks, there would be no Barrister. It's this distinction that Cliff tries in vain to suppress to his subconscious. He lives by the "ends justifying the means" cliché. Nonetheless, the game must have its players. "Would you excuse me for one second?" Cliff excuses himself.

Logan approaches Cliff. "Logan. Good of you to come," Cliff forces out.

"Wouldn't miss it." Logan replies. Cliff forces a smile as he shakes Logan's hand, but not too tightly. "It's been a while since we chatted. We should do lunch," Logan offers.

"Yes. You should call Grace to set it up," Cliff says.

"Or you could just pick up the phone every once in a while," Logan jousts. Cliff smirks and sips from his glass.

"Cell phones don't work at Barrister, Logan. You know that," Cliff retorts. Logan frowns at Cliff. The air is thick enough to cut with a knife.

Cliff can't deny he's been dodging Logan for some time now. It's human nature to avoid unpleasantness in all of its forms. Cliff hates himself for taking their money in the first place. He lied to himself that he could still do great things, in spite of their reputation to exploit research for warfare. But even Cliff can't escape his chains. Mercifully, Rachel, Cliff's beautiful wife of over twenty years, and the institute's chief animal biologist, strolls in their direction. Cliff smiles widely. Logan, who knows Cliff's avoidance moves well, turns to identify his distraction.

Rachel is a radiant beauty in her late 40s. And in her dress plays more to a fashion model than a Forensic Anthropologist. Tonight she is playing the role of gracious host. She knows full well of Cliff's distaste with the expectations that come from suckling on the corporate teat, but she does as much as she can to help her beloved husband deflect his loathing. If only to save political face. She embraces Cliff warmly. Almost as if to pacify him and keep him from making a scene. "Great turn out," she says.

"Wonderful. You remember Logan Gibson from Hicks?" he replies. The question is a PC formality since he is well aware of her knowledge of the man. He is often the topic of dinner time conversations. Rachel turns to Logan gracefully. She offers her hand. Logan receives it as if complying with cultural protocol. The trio are simply going through the motions like politicians eager to get each other's votes while slapping each other simultaneously. The games we play.

"Of course. How are you Logan?" she asks sincerely.

"Fine, thank you," Logan replies. Logan knows the score, but also has tremendous respect for both Cliff and Rachel. Rachel turns back to Cliff.

"How was the lecture? I missed most of it following up with a necropsy in med lab," Rachel inquires.

"Good enough to scare up some donations I'm sure," Logan interjects. The trio laugh at the irony of the joke. Of course Hicks is the primary source of money here and everyone knows it. And Logan doesn't particularly care for being ignored when he's responsible for paying the bills. So you get your jabs in while you can.

Cliff surveys the room and spies Jack by the back wall. The opportunity to escape the sadistic torture of talking to Logan has finally presented itself. Cliff jumps on it with wide eyes. "Rachel, darling, it's time you met my protégé." Cliff directs with a smile. "Excuse us." He tosses at Logan. Rachel breathes a sigh of relief at the moment and gladly takes Cliff's arm. Logan smirks at being cast aside yet again. It's gotten pretty old. Cliff and Rachel stroll away.

"Call me." Logan warns. Cliff waves at Logan without looking back, in his patronizing way. Their game is just getting started.

Cliff and Rachel stroll up to Jack. Jack, not expecting the meet and greet, straightens up and attempts to make his attire look less inappropriate than it is. His muscles tighten up. He may be a rebel without a cause at heart, but this still caught him by surprise.

"Dr. Barrister, Mrs. Barrister," Jack half mumbles through the nerves. Cliff smirks.

"Come on Jack, you're practically family. Call me Cliff," Cliff responds.

"Call me Rachel," Rachel adds as she extends her hand gracefully. Jack smiles warmly and receives it. Cliff spies Jack's attire awkwardly.

"You didn't read the invitation?" Cliff asks with almost an embarrassed-for-Jack tone with a half smile.Jack looks himself over as if for the first time. It will take some quick thinking to get out of this one alive, Jack thinks.

"You were serious about that? Actually this is the closest thing I have to semi-formal. Graduate student, remember?" Jack playfully declares, very proud of himself for crushing the improvisation. Cliff smiles.

"Don't you worry Jack. Cliff's just jealous he didn't think of it," Rachel answers with a wink. Jack lets out a small relieved sigh. That situation wasn't too awkward.

Beth Barrister, Cliff and Rachel's only child, approaches the group. "Hi, mom," Beth semi interrupts. Jack's eyes widen. Rachel embraces Beth warmly.

"There you are. I've been looking all over for you," Rachel pronounces. Jack stares at Beth with wide eyes. His nerves have suddenly kicked in again. The last thing he expected at this reception was to come face to face with the girl he was head over heels for in high school. Talk about your small world. Jack suddenly feels the universe is out to get him. But in a good way.Now he just has to handle this situation with poise. Way more poise than he did with Cliff. Cliff sees Jack's reaction. Cliff is no dummy. He is well aware of Jack's feelings. In his own twisted way, Cliff hopes to take advantage of that, albeit in the lab.

"Honey, you remember Jackson Hart?" Cliff offers. Beth gazes at Jack. Of course she remembers him, but that was high school. And he was a bit Magoo back then. No, let's face it, he was downright awkward. Interestingly enough for Beth, she likes awkward. Not that she'd ever admit it to herself, let alone Jack. Jack smiles at Beth.

"Hi," he says, hoping to make a good impression. Beth studies him for a long second.

"No, I don't," Beth responds to Rachel's question. Jack's smile withers slowly and embarrassingly.

"We knew each other in high school," Jack reveals as if trying to convince himself as much as remind Beth.

"Oh." Beth smiles with wide eyes, looking a bit like Helen Hunt trying to laugh at Mel Gibson in What Women Want.

"Jack is doing his graduate work at the institute this year," Cliff advises in a negotiating tone. Cliff sees the writing on the wall. Beth is not going to make this easy for him.

"Good," Beth replies, understanding her father's message and dialing down the hostility a bit.

"Beth has been doing bacterial research in Africa for the CDC the past four months," Cliff declares proudly to Jack. Not that Jack needs to be more impressed.

"Awesome," Jack says, smiling wide as if answering the cue to be impressed. Beth smiles awkwardly at her father's attempt to feed the stalker. She shoots Cliff a "please stop" smirk.

"Jack is doing cutting edge work over at the University, and I thought you two would work very well together," Cliff suggests. Beth's eyes widen at Cliff.

"Did you?" Beth replies with an accusatory tone at her father's cupid like gesture. Cliff smiles proudly and nods affirmative. He enjoys the game of torturing his baby girl, especially when romance is the topic. Rachel feels the temperature of the conversation rising, and takes action.

"Jack, there is someone I'd like you to meet," Rachel announces. She loops her hand under Jack's arm stealthily and leads him away from the conversation. Beth stares awkwardly at Cliff, her eyes burning like a laser.

"What are you doing?" Beth accuses.

"Nothing," Cliff defends. But of course he's doing something. They all have a role to play in this game. Beth looks crossly at Cliff.

"Why?" she pleads. Cliff's demeanor changes to a more relaxed tone.

"He's the most advanced student I've ever seen. He's being published next month on morphology. We need him Beth. You know that," Cliff summarizes in a matter of fact tone. Cliff speaks in double entendres. Beth knows the institute needs a breakthrough. That much is obvious. But Cliff needs a little lightning to strike to appease Hicks. He keeps that from his family. No need to concern them about things out of their control. Beth sighs heavily and looks away. She understands the need is great, and knows she has a role to play in the family business. It doesn't mean she has to like it.

"High school?" Beth retorts. Cliff smiles.

"Maybe he still has a crush on you," Cliff jokes. Beth rolls her eyes and smiles. Cliff reciprocates.

CHAPTER 2

Waterston University has been a stalwart institution of higher learning since the early 20s.It's never reached Ivy League status, but it's graduated some of the finest minds in medicine, technology and science. The areas of study include micro organisms, both known and unknown. Applications include the areas of medicine, bio tech and practical application science. In 2005, at the height of the latest discovery from the Barrister Institute, Waterston University created an internship program to allow students to achieve graduate credits in exchange for hands on lab work in the research and development of some of the most fascinating discoveries of the 21st century. Dr. Cliff Barrister and his wife Rachel also began the Barrister scholarship program which funds five extraordinary students' educations each year at Waterston. The science lab at Waterston was almost exclusively paid for from Governmental Grants along with The Barrister Fund for Higher Learning. Some of the school's high profile alumni include high ranking scientists at the CDC, US Department of Energy, as well as a Secretary of State and several corporate officers at pharmaceutical companies.

Not coincidentally, Jack has attended the school the past 2 years on the Barrister scholarship and in his senior year was surprised as a late addition to the internship program at Barrister. Jack's morphology study was recognized by the CDC and the White House and has Jack on the fast track to any number of high profile science, pharmaceutical or even university teaching positions. He's 21 years old and is on pace to be one of the youngest doctorate graduates in history. That is if he can mature outside the classroom a bit.

The science lab at Waterston is a large wing of the Barrister Science building which includes 20 dual student workstations outfitted with tables, chemistry equipment and computers all connected to the high power microscope which the class uses, among other things, to study ice core samples donated by the National Ice Core Laboratory.

Jack slumps at his station, joined by his lab partner Barry. They're feeling the effects of their shenanigans at the lecture the evening before, as well as the libations. Between the jack hammer going off in his temples and weight of his eyelids, Jack is both sorry he got up this morning and elated at the adventure. Being one of the smartest people in the room can make life boring, like Gulliver in his travels. But as Murphy's Law would suggest, just when you're comfortable that the world won't change, you wake up on Lilliput. Jack slips on his sunglasses in the hopes of drowning out the roar of life around him, if only briefly.

The classroom door opens and Professor Jones saunters through it. A celebrated scientist in his own right, Jones is a 57 year old published author and Fulbright Scholar. A scientific grant allowed the African born professor to study in his homeland as a young man, and his work while there paved the way for the current water well program which brings fresh water to outlying areas less likely to find life sustaining resources. His influence was one of the reasons Jack chose Waterston to conduct his graduate studies. That and Jack appreciates Jones' no nonsense approach to learning.

"Good morning people. The life of a scientist is filled with boredom with the exception of those few moments you manage to make a discovery, get published or change humanity forever.

With any luck some of you will," Jones preaches. Jack lets out a gastrointestinal groan, unable to control himself. "You have something to add today Mr. Hart?" Jones inquires sarcastically. Jack waves him away. Jones smiles and shakes his head. "If you applied your energy to your studies with the same vigor as your extracurricular activities, you could change the world," Jones summates. Jack peeks his bloodshot eyes out from behind his glasses and smiles faintly at the gesture, like someone who lost this battle but has every intention of winning the war. Jones continues, "We have a unique opportunity this morning. We were granted access to a new ice core sample courtesy of the National Ice Core Laboratory, which came from the latest sample taken from the Antarctic Ice Shelf. If you've kept up with your current events, worldwide ice shelf erosion is a problem. This sample is from among the deepest samples ever extracted. Meaning you will be seeing material no one else has ever seen. So pay attention."

This grabs Jack's attention. He removes his glasses, ignoring the alcohol induced gorilla pounding on his head and sits up. Jones powers up the microscope from his computer. Bill and Maggie, a pair of upper classmen, enter the clean room and grab a pair of suits. They look like astronauts or deep sea explorers as they seal each other's suits. The need for a clean environment is taken as seriously here at Waterston as it is at the CDC. In fact, they report new findings to the CDC on a regular basis, making it one of the leading colleges in the nation for both doctors and deadly disease scientists. Jack gazes intently at the process, like an armchair quarterback making sure the play is executed correctly. Perhaps that's one of Jack's OCD qualities.

Bill and Maggie enter the freezer and open a storage unit at the center of the room. The freezer houses a series of storage units that contain everything from ice core samples to tissue samples for study. Bill slowly retrieves a Styrofoam container from the storage unit and carefully carries it to a workstation near the microscope loading platform. He inches it along ever so slowly, as if it were nitroglycerin. "Bill, be careful with that. Maggie, help him load it in the microscope," Jones instructs. Maggie gives him the thumbs up. She has an intercom but she is not a fan of using it on account of not liking how she sounds when she hears herself. That always makes Jack chuckle a bit. Maggie joins Bill at the work station. Bill removes the lid very carefully and inches out a tube containing the ice core sample. He softly lays it on the table and rotates the lid on one end. Classmates watch from the observation window with the intensity of watching a horror movie. Maggie holds the tube in place as Bill gently removes the long cylinder of ice. The structural integrity of the sample is not in question, but given its rarity, if it's dropped and broken, anything of scientific value they find would be called into question. So they treat the sample with more care than the Crown Jewels. Bill and Maggie, each holding an end of the sample, slowly place it on the cradle attached to the microscope.

Jones types feverishly on the computer. As he does, small clamps at three intervals of the ice core tray close and softly clamp down on the sample and the tray slowly glides on the track toward the microscope's mouth as if swallowing a popsicle.

Jack watches intently as the ice core sample disappears from view. Monitors in the classroom spring to life with images from within the microscope. Bill and Maggie high five one another to celebrate another completed mission and exit back to the clean room to remove their suits. The classroom monitors illuminate with a rotating image of the ice core sample as chemical and biological data begins scrolling down the left side of the screen. Jones watches the data and smiles. "OK people, let's get to work," Jones instructs. Students scatter to their workstations. Jones types feverishly on his computer. Different sections of the sample show up on monitors all over the classroom. Students open notebooks and write feverishly. Others open laptops and open virtual text books, charts and table of elements.

Computer monitors dance with information. Students watch in fascination, writing in their notebooks feverishly. They type on their computers to get different views of their samples and study chemical compositions. Jones speaks to students and points to different elements to pay attention to. Jones really loves teaching these kids. In some ways it's more satisfying than working in science. Molding minds into tomorrow's leaders. Very few get that chance.

Jack studies the sample in front of him and Barry. The image rotates and the data scrolls the screen. Suddenly a large spot appears with a red blinking message that catches Jack's attention. He types on his computer to isolate that spot. The image enlarges in 3D and rotates. Jack types information to ask the computer to identify the material. An error message interrupts him. Jack turns his head slightly and looks at Barry. He types new commands. Same error. Jack opens a new screen and types the chemical composition into a search engine. "No matches found," replies the computer.

"Professor?" Jack inquires. Jones looks up as Jack waves him over. He strolls over to Jack and Barry's table. Jack looks at Jones and points to the spot. Jones puts on his reading glasses and spies the screen carefully. He touches Jack on the shoulder and Jack shoots out of his seat. Jones plops down and types feverishly at the computer. The same error message greets the professor. Jones types several more options, each meeting with the same harsh electronic response. This material is not ready to give up its secrets quite yet. Jones types in a command to diagnostically analyze the spot. The computer ponders the request for several nail-biting seconds. The air becomes a little thick as Jack eagerly awaits the revelation of just what they've found. Finally, the computer dashes their hopes with a chemical readout followed by "NOT PREVIOUSLY RECORDED".

"It looks like a single cell microbe," Jack hypothesizes.

"It's definitely a microbe of some kind. Apparently a rarely seen one," Jones concedes. Jones commands the computer to print a list of known microbes from ice core samples. The printer hums and spits out the list. Jones yanks the answer off the printer and studies the results. Jack studies the computer image like a peeping tom. Jones sighs. "I have no idea what this is," Jones confesses. Jack looks back at Jones surprised with a half smile like he just found a silver dollar. But Jack has bigger aspirations than a payday. He sees a quick trip to fame if he's discovered something brand new. This gives Jack an idea.

"I have access to everything we need at Barrister. I can study it and find out what it is," Jack offers. Jones looks at Jack. Even though he can see right through his bright student's intentions, Jack has a point. And hell, if he's discovered the find of the century, why not give the kid a chance to prove it. Not to mention, as his teacher and a long time scientist, it would prove an amazing thing to be associated with Jack for his career as well. Not that he cares that much about fame for himself. But it gives him pride to see his student take some ambitious chances. Jones looks at the image and back at Jack.

"Maybe you'll change the world after all Mr. Hart," Jones encourages. Jack smiles like a kid in a candy store. He looks back at the computer screen as the message "NOT PREVIOUSLY RECORDED" continues to rotate. Jack is going to find out what this material is. But he's not going to like it.

CHAPTER 3

The campus where the Barrister Institute is housed was built by the Center for Disease Control and Prevention back in the early 70s and was a state of the art research facility. It was supposed to be a supplementary research facility to the Atlanta hub. During the mid 80s, budget cuts to the CDC forced some closures, including the Texas campus. As a way of resurrecting the facility, the CDC donated it to the Barristers in 1987 as more of a public relations move as well as unloading some of the headaches that came along with the upkeep and security of the grounds. But the move would be well served as the Barristers would breathe new life into the facility, using grants from several branches of the government as well as private donations to upgrade the site to modern times.

During the early days of the institute, several high profile finds, both biological and technical, brought international attention to the Barristers. Barristers has also been known for the development of an early warning system for illnesses and outbreaks. They've even been credited with saving thousands of lives from their forecasts and warnings that have stemmed outbreaks in a dozen countries. This talent earned the Barristers respect in the field and brought more high profile investors including Hicks Corporation, a pharmaceutical giant with rumored links to the Department of Energy and Department of Defense in Washington. There has never been a solid link between them, but some of the contracts Hicks has received from those agencies forced questions of the true relationship between them. Hicks' interest in Barrister and the institute have always been widely rumored for everything from money laundering to biological weapons development. No concrete evidence has ever been found however, and it all remains rumor and conjecture.

In recent years the new finds have slowed or stopped. Fame is like a firecracker. It burns hot but only lasts a short time and then you need another one to continue the burn or you risk nobody watching anymore.

This revelation is not lost on Cliff. He never wanted this. He wanted to make a difference in the world. He and Rachel started out as idealists in a realist world. The lessons of how life really is are hard for most. The simple fact is the world revolves around money and power in one way or another. There is no escaping it. The only way around it is through it. Cliff has understood that for some time now. As the years have worn on, and the discoveries have slowed down or stopped altogether, relationships the Barristers have enjoyed over this many years are going the way of the firecracker, and they know it.

Cliff and Rachel have made a difference in the world. Policies are in place in countries around the world thanks to their discoveries in the areas of disease prevention, catastrophe protocol and other areas. They've left a lasting legacy in that regard. But Cliff isn't an old man yet. He has years more to give. He has no intention of letting everything they've built together just fall by the wayside. But adjusting to this new reality of the love for money has also taken its toll on Cliff. He is no longer an idealist. Some days he wrestles with pessimism in his quest to only remain a realist. But he also knows something has to change. Or he will go down in history as "that guy that did that thing that one time". Cliff can think of nothing more tragic.

This was one of the driving factors of Cliff offering an advanced internship to Jackson Hart. Cliff has been a scientist for a long time, and he has never met a sharper intellect and problem solver than Jack. He hates to admit it, but Jack reminds him of himself as a young man, but a smarter version, if that's possible. He knows the spark they need at Barrister is someone who can come in and either create a brand new discovery or stumble upon it. They need someone with the vision to realize they have something and to bring it to Barrister. The fact that Jack and his daughter Beth had a nerdish type romance in high school can only help that along. If nature takes its course, both figuratively and literally, Jack can bring so much to the family. Perhaps even take the reigns as the scientist heir apparent. But let's not get ahead of ourselves, Cliff fantasizes. It's not Cliff's intention to use him, or to take advantage of a situation for his own personal advancement. That's what it really is, but Cliff thinks of it in bigger picture terms. The ends justify the means. But first things first. It's all a moot point if Jack finds nothing. The ship is slowly sinking and Cliff knows it. Even Rachel, in her own way, knows it. They don't talk about it. But it's there like a dark cloud hovering over them. And Logan is the proverbial vulture waiting for them to produce or die.

The microbiology lab at Barrister was one area where no expense was spared. If you want to make the big discoveries, you can't be cheap in your equipment. One of Cliff's sayings. The 2000 square foot lab features a walk-in freezer, clean room, computer control room and break room along with the powerful microscope and incinerator. Jack, Cliff and Beth review a monitor displaying the findings Jack recorded to a CD at Waterston. Cliff stares blankly at the screen. On a separate computer he types a new search of his own but his results are just as empty as Jack's. Beth runs her own search with the same results. They look at Jack with wide eyes. "Any ideas?" Jack inquires. Cliff looks over at Jack, sighs and raises his eyebrows.

"No," Cliff replies stoically, trying to hide his hope that this could be something, anything. But again, let's not get ahead of ourselves. Beth looks at them both. Jack smiles like a kid who just found a silver dollar.

"Let's find out what it is," Jack begs. Cliff sighs like he's not thoroughly enjoying this moment. And Jack is doing all the work. Of course he wants to find out what this is but looking desperate is not an option. It may turn out to be nothing, but it's the best lead he's had in months.

"Alright, I'll write it up. Get to work you two," Cliff advises. Beth's head whips around at Cliff as if shot out of a gun.

"I need to finish my report," Beth objects. Beth sees right through Cliff. She expected he'd have her do some research or something, not be his lab partner.

"That can wait. Let's work on this first," Cliff subtly negotiates. The father and daughter dynamic in full swing. Beth need not enjoy the time she spends with Jack, but Cliff wants to know as soon as possible if this will be helpful. And the one person he trusts with that revelation is Beth. Beth gets it. But she hates it. She glares at Cliff. Cliff stares back. Beth sighs and walks away.

"Everything OK?" Jack asks, feeling the ever thickening air in the room. Cliff smiles and pats Jack on the shoulder like it's not Jack's fault that he has no idea the gravity of the question. Too many things going on simultaneously to even start that conversation, Cliff thinks. He walks away. Jack follows him out of the room with his eyes. Jack knows something's up, and assumes it must be him.

"Keep me posted," Cliff instructs very matter-of-factly.

"OK," Jack responds. Jack sits at the computer terminal and types.

Beth strolls in and sighs. The moment she has been trying to avoid has finally arrived. She thought after high school she would be able to walk away from the feelings she had for Jack. His naivety and shyness were cute for a while. But his obliviousness to her feelings proved a bit harder to get over. She's a very pretty girl. And he should have appreciated it a bit more. But that's all in the past now. The duties of being a Barrister call, and she will do as is required of her and see what Jack has found.

"Alright, let's get this over with. I authored a paper on new organism research and created a bio protocol to test materials," Beth advises.

"Did you?" Jack replies, clearly impressed. Jack is not as good at hiding his feelings as he wants to be. He was always impressed with Beth. He always felt unworthy of her affections though, so telling her how he felt was out of the question. But expressing his feelings in other ways, like celebrating her victories, is completely within his comfort zone. Beth glares back at Jack, assuming his tone is meant as sarcasm instead of sincerity.

"That a problem?" she accuses. Jack smiles big.

"Nope," he says.

"We expose the material to biological and elemental compounds to gauge reaction. We document which materials react favorably. Which ones kill the organism. Whatever. Once that's done, we can make a genetic map of it and submit the results to the CDC for confirmation and recording," Beth explains.

"Impressive," Jack says as if expressing his love for her. Beth smiles faintly, picking up the subtle cue and allowing herself a brief moment to enjoy the affection.

"Thanks," she replies, both to the statement and the sentiment.

Beth types feverishly on the computer. Screens from her software flash and scroll in a dance of light with her as its conductor. Machines in the server room bleep and hum into action. The microscope jumps to life in a series of small mechanical arm maneuvers inside the clean room. The arm opens a freezer door, retrieves the sample container and eloquently removes the sample from its container, placing it on the workstation table next to it. A laser arm protrudes out and slithers over the top of the sample like a snake hunting its prey. The laser slices a wafer thin section of the ice core sample free. Another small arm follows that and removes the sliver of ice from the workstation and places it gently on a tray. Then as if working with precious material, lightly slides the tray into the microscope and seals the opening. It backs slowly away, its task completed. Computer monitors spring to life with data in three dimensional images of the sample with scrolling data as the ice gives up its secrets. A separate monitor vomits the chemical composition of the compounds and organic material it sees in the microscope. The first compound on the list highlights. "How long is this going to take?" Jake inquires.

"I dunno. This is the first time I've run it," Beth replies. Jack peeks at his watch.

"Do we have time to eat?" Jack asks. Beth looks at Jack as if he just asked her on a date. She reels in her emotional response, considering he has a point. They need to eat and this analysis could take a while. She rises and they head out of the room as the monitors work tirelessly behind them.

CHAPTER 4

Jack and Beth enter the Barrister Institute cafeteria. An impressive eatery by any standards, it includes an enormous kitchen with 6 stations that serve a variety of foods from standard American fare in addition to Chinese food, pizza, Italian, Vegan and Mexican along with a coffee bar. The cafeteria is large enough to house the entire institute's staff with 50 tables with chairs. Entrances from both the east and west wing make it easy to get to. Beth nibbles a salad as Jack takes a bite out of his turkey on rye sandwich.

"The CDC, huh?" Jack inquires in a tone both designed to praise the accomplishment as much as weaken the ice between them. Beth looks up from her salad receiving the double entendre gesture. "What you did in Africa?" Jack continues, making sure the message was delivered. Jack never was any good at picking up subtle hints.

"Yeah," Beth responds, half toying with Jack and half sincerely thankful he noticed.

"E. Coli?" Jack asks, probing for conversation. In spite of the history between them, they are actually very comfortable with each other. Beth hates that worse than anything. She sighs.

"Salmonella risk factors in infants," she replies, afraid of Jack's reaction. She wants to say it again in a different tone because she can feel her wall cracking just a bit.

"I knew you'd change the world," Jack compliments her. Beth stops chewing. Jack is really trying to connect with her and she feels it. Maybe he's grown up a bit since last they saw each other. She plays with her food nervously pondering her next move.

"What about you?" she asks, changing the subject.

"Nothing so noble. Though I do have a mean recipe for moonshine," Jack responds. His self-depreciative tone attempting to keep the spotlight on Beth. He has no shortage of self-confidence, even a bit of arrogance about his abilities, but this is not the time nor the place. Beth smiles at the gesture. She senses that he's trying.

"Moonshine?" she pokes. Her gesture of cracking the door ajar gets Jack's attention. Now don't screw it up, he thinks. Jack smiles.

"I get bored easily," he replies.

"That would explain your 4.0 average," Beth jokes again. Jack stops chewing his most recent bite and looks at Beth and smiles big. They are actually having a conversation now. This is progress. Jack sees an opening and takes it.

"If only I'd been that smart in high school," Jack says. His undertone of regret for not expressing his feelings sooner on display. Beth smiles at his confession. Though she's not quite ready to go there yet. But she is enjoying the conversation.

"This bacteria you've found may be an important find," Beth says, changing the subject both to get their relationship off topic but also to restore his confidence.

"Maybe," Jack replies hopefully.

Out of the corner of her eye, Beth notices Jason approach the table. Jason is a rather hunky, but cocky 22 year old in his senior year of internship from the university. For the past 18 months, he's served under Dr. Barrister as the lead intern on most projects. The status he's enjoyed has gone to his head. He's still a very bright young man, but he's become more in love with the power than the science. And Beth feels the heat of his thoughts on the back of her neck every time he talks to her. She tolerates it because they are co-workers now. But he's slick as old motor oil.

"Hi Beth," Jason gleefully chimes. Beth looks up at Jason and forces a smile.

"Jason. How are you?" Beth politely replies, using the most worn greeting of all time. Jason smiles at the thought she's thought about him. But of course she has. Why wouldn't she?

"Good. Looking forward to tonight," Jason flirts. As subtlety goes, it's not Jason's strong suit. He doesn't need it most of the time. He's quite the ladies' man. Just ask him. Beth's face flushes at the overtone.

"Yeah. Should be fun. This is Jackson Hart," Beth says, changing the awkward subject. Jack picks up on the cue but unaware of the strike about to be launched in his direction. Jason speaks without taking his eyes off Beth.

"Resident genius. I know," he says with a hint of competition and a sprinkle of contempt. Jack suddenly feels the target on his chest, making him take a semi-deep breath. Jack looks up at Jason, trying to recall what he said or did to warrant such a hostile reception. Jason feels the eyes on the side of his face and glances over at Jack. Standing at the table like a warrior staring down at his target from an elevated position. Jack offers his hand in half truce. Jason receives it out of pure politically correct protocol, as if doing Jack a favor he didn't earn.

"Nice to meet you," Jack offers weakly, still trying to track the missile of hostility to its point of origin. Jason smiles.

"Dr. Barrister speaks highly of you. So highly he gave you my internship," Jason retorts. The truth comes out. Jack's face flushes like it was covered in a hot blanket as he recognizes the sharp edge of envy that just cut him. Jack never considered the consequences of his good fortune would mean something bad for someone else. A miscalculation that's created a pretty awkward situation. "I'm sorry," Jack apologizes, knowing it would have no effect. But social politics demand their protocol nonetheless.

"Don't be. I'm sure you're all that," Jason warns. Whether Jack likes it or not, his very existence has earned him an enemy, at least for now. Nothing to be done or said. Jason looks at his watch like he's become suddenly bored with the conversation. He has to end the conversation on his terms, after all, in order to show Jack what he's up against. "I gotta go," Jason advises. He looks at Beth and smiles. "See you tonight," he continues. Jack feels the warning to stay away from romantic inclinations as they apply to Beth. Whether he feels them or not. Beth smiles awkwardly. Jason trots away.

The air has been sucked out of the room. But with it a sense of relief. Beth breaks the awkward silence. "They're throwing me a welcome back party at Joe's," Beth says.

"He's sure glad to have you back," Jack offers sarcastically, trying not to completely avoid the elephant in the room. Beth shifts in her seat uncomfortably. She'd prefer not to think about that.

"Why don't you come?" she offers, almost surprising herself. Jack glances in Jason's general direction. He's just getting started around here and though he can't hide his feelings for Beth forever, perhaps attending a function with Jason around may prove a bigger challenge than he really wants to deal with right now. Not to mention Jason would probably take him in a fight. Probably should wait as long as possible for that confrontation.

"I should finish the analysis," Jack replies. His words pierce the air like an arrow and suck the remaining momentum their previous conversation had right out of the air. Perhaps Jack hasn't grown up that much after all, Beth thinks. She shakes her head hiding her regret.

"Yeah," she replies.

CHAPTER 5

Jack has spent many evenings in the Barrister lab late at night working on projects, research papers or just to clear his head. This time it's different. He senses the awkwardness between he and Beth. More to the point, when he gets close to something good, there are always obstacles. His internship. His relationships. Even his parents, who shipped him off to schools he didn't want to go to because he was so smart. They told him it was for his own good in order for him to develop. But he just wanted to be a kid. It's as if adulthood was thrust on him against his will from a young age. Maybe that's why he goes out of his way to play games now. So much is expected from him that he never asked for. He didn't ask to be so smart. But here he is with the burden to carry.

Jack slumps in a chair in the lab, which is devoid of light. The monitors dance with result after result of "No Reaction" as the organism goes through test after test. Jack is beginning to believe, like all good things he's ever wanted, this will come to nothing. The monitors, so far, support his theory. Jack reaches into his wallet and pulls out the only picture in it. It's Beth. The only girl he ever really cared for. How ironic it is that she's suddenly back in his life but seemingly further away than ever. He stares at the picture and sighs at the ridiculous random nature of things.

A beep on the monitor behind him breaks his attention from the picture. He glances over his shoulder and sees an entry that's blinking on the screen. He turns to address the console directly. He flips on the lights and his eyes widen. Holy shit. "What the fuck?" he delightfully exclaims. They got a fusing reaction from Zinc Beryllium Silicate. Jack types feverishly as the printers spring to life behind him. Data spits out of the printer. Jack eyeballs it. He's never seen anything like it before. And he's pretty sure nobody else has either. Perhaps this is not as much of a disaster as he thought. Jack will work all through the night analyzing the data.

As the sun peeks through the blinds to welcome in the morning, Beth strolls through the lab entrance. Hair still wet from her shower she slows her pace as she approaches Jack, who types at the console. Jack sees her behind him. "Good, you're here," he exclaims. She stops next to him.

"Weren't you wearing that shirt yesterday?" she inquires. Jack doesn't even hear the question. "You didn't go home last night," she continues. Jack stands up and looks at Beth with a huge grin. He suddenly grabs her and kisses her on the lips. Her eyes bulge with surprise and delight. She knows he kissed her for a reason, and she's sure the reason's important. But she enjoyed it all the same. "What?" she asks. Jack excitedly hands her a printout. The forward thinking move of kissing her hasn't reached his brain yet, and no time to reflect at the moment, especially after pulling an all nighter.

Beth reads the paper and her eyes widen slowly. "This doesn't make any sense," she concludes. Jack finishes the thought for her.

"No results until it was exposed to Zinc Beryllium Silicate," he says.

"It fused? What does that even mean?" she probes. Jack types on a keyboard. The monitor flashes a three dimensional molecular model of the compound ZnMBe. Beth studies it in disbelief.

"The bacteria fused itself to the compound. It's a stable, bio-elemental compound," Jack advises with confidence.

"That's not possible," Beth concludes, her brain still trying to wrap itself around this crazy idea.

"Wasn't possible yesterday. It is today." Jack shrugs with a cute little cockiness that he knows he's on to something never before found. In his sleep deprived state he comes across a little like he's drunk. Beth and Jack gaze at each other and then at the monitor. They are both aware that this is going to be a huge find. It's both exciting and scary at the same time.

CHAPTER 6

Jack and Beth briskly enter Cliff's office. It's rather small by corporate standards. At fifteen feet long and twelve feet wide, it's comfortable for Cliff. He doesn't spend that much time in it anyway. He sits at a seven foot by four foot mahogany desk. Overkill for Cliff, but Rachel insisted. Two chairs rest in front of it, but it could easily hold three. A floor to ceiling bookshelf looms over the room on one side while the wall behind Cliff's desk has a bay window overlooking the courtyard. The third wall has an entry to Med Lab. Cliff humorously thinks of it as "the escape hatch".

Cliff is on the phone behind his desk as Jack and Beth enter. Cliff doesn't notice them and his phone is on speaker. "Hicks Pharmaceuticals has been an ally of The Barrister Institute since your work on elemental fusion efficiency was published ten years ago. That's why Hicks has proudly continued support for your research. That's why I don't want to do this on the phone," Logan summarizes. Cliff sighs. He so loathes having to play politics. Not only is it boring but it keeps him from doing what he loves. And Logan is just a hack anyway.

"Alright, I'll have Grace check my schedule," Cliff says to placate Logan. Logan senses it of course.

"I'll see you soon," he replies. Cliff takes his frustration out on the hang-up button.

Beth clears her throat. Cliff looks up surprised. Jack and Beth stare at Cliff like they just made him breakfast in bed. "What?" Cliff inquires with a half smile.He knows that look and that's almost always good news.

"We need you to come to the lab. We have something to show you. Bring mom." Beth smiles. Cliff rises in one motion from his chair as if lifted in zero gravity. He opens the door to Med Lab quickly.

"Rachel. Come here. Beth has something to show us," Cliff commands excitedly. Rachel stops what she's doing, removes her lab coat and exits the Med Lab through Cliff's office. They briskly walk out of the room and down the hall to the lab like they're on their way to Christmas morning.

"What's going on?" Rachel asks.

"We'll show you," Beth says smiling.

They enter the lab and Jack brings them to the monitor with the compound and its data. Rachel and Cliff look the screen over carefully. "A bio-elemental compound?" Cliff asks with a dumbfounded look. He's never seen anything like it, and that's saying a lot. He looks at Rachel. Jack shakes his head yes like he nailed an answer on Jeopardy. Rachel shrugs her shoulders. Beth smiles. "You're sure about this?" Cliff asks Jack.

"Checked it three times," Jack replies confidently with a smile.

"I also checked it," Beth continues matter-of-factly. Not that they don't believe Jack, but couldn't hurt that their daughter agrees. Cliff looks them over and shrugs his shoulders, giving them the why not gesture.

Jason enters the lab and stops at the powwow that's taking place. "Jack, let's test this theory of yours. Jason, run the standard battery of bio tests," Cliff commands. Jason glares at Jack. Not only is this asshole taking his internship, he's cock blocking with

Beth and has Cliff wrapped around his finger? Hell no. But he's gotta play the long game.

"Yes, Dr. Barrister," Jason responds with a smile.

"Let's see what this thing can do," Cliff says.

Jason types at the console. Jack and Beth enter the clean room and suit up. Smiles agape. They enter the freezer. They retrieve the container with the sample and place it on the steel work station. They open a refrigerator and claim a plastic container. Beth syringes small amounts of the compound on a large piece of glass split into fifty sections. Jack follows and syringes samples of organic matter onto each piece behind her. They place the glass on the microscope and exit the clean room. Jason types and monitors dance with data. The monotone of the microscope motor whirs silently.

Jack and Beth enter the lab again and they huddle around the monitors. A light on the microscope control panel illuminates bright red. This grabs the group's attention. "We got something," Cliff announces. Jack studies the monitor.

"It's the blood samples," Jack reveals.

"What type?" Cliff asks.

"All of them," Rachel chimes in. Cliff looks up at Rachel and then at Jack. This was not something any of them expected. This compound gets more mysterious with each question they answer. Cliff won't admit it yet but he is starting to get the feeling this material may be what he's been looking for. If it is, he's not sure that's a good thing.

The monitor announces "TEST COMPLETE". Cliff sighs. "Fifty biological compounds and the only thing it responded to was blood samples," Cliff summarizes. Rachel looks at Cliff like he's announcing aliens. She's never seen anything like this, and it worries her a little bit. Beth studies the image of the blood and types on the console to transfer the image to the monitor.

"What is it doing?" she asks nervously. Rachel looks up at the monitor.

"What do you make of that?" Cliff inquires. Rachel studies the image and sighs heavily.

"I think it's feeding," she advises, trying to hide her concern. She's a scientist, and this should be an exciting moment. But for some reason, it's not.

"Like staph?" Cliff inquires, trying to wrap his brain around it. Rachel nods yes. Anything that feeds on blood samples is something they need to take seriously, she thinks.

"But there's something else," she answers. She points to the monitor. "These were stored samples, right?" she continues.

"Yes," Jack responds. Rachel sits at the console and types feverishly, her brain clearly working the problem.

"We need a live subject," she insists.

"Why?" Cliff asks.

"This compound isn't built like Staph. It's at least part synthetic. But it seems to react to blood in a similar way to Staph. The only way to do a live comparison is to use a live specimen," Rachel advises.

Cliff looks over at Jason. "We need a couple of specimens. Let's use a mouse and an ape," Cliff requests. Jason scribbles the note on a notepad and bolts out of the room.

"Have you already run containment protocol?" Rachel inquires.

"Not yet," Cliff answers. Beth looks oddly at Jack.

"What's containment protocol?" she asks.

"We never test on live subjects until we know how to contain the material first," Jack replies. Beth knows the answer to the question but asks it anyway since this whole thing feels surreal.

"Contain it?" she asks.

"Kill it," Jack replies.

There is a heightened tenseness in the air. This material is clearly a huge find. One none of them expected. At the same time, until they know what they're dealing with, you have to treat it with respect. The minute you don't, it could go very badly. Cliff types repeatedly on the console. A robotic arm in the clean room removes the tray from the microscope. Rachel enters the clean room and puts on a protective suit. She unlocks a locker on the far wall.

"She uses a dozen chemical agents. Whichever of them kills the material, we keep handy when testing on the animals. Just in case," Jack educates Beth. Rachel retrieves a cooler from the refrigerator and places it on the table. She opens it slowly to reveal a panel of syringes of various colors. She removes each syringe and places small amounts of its contents on the compound samples. Cliff studies the monitor. The compound shows no ill effects from any of the chemicals. Cliff knows this isn't right. These are toxins being applied to the material. Something should have an effect on it. Cliff eyes Rachel through the observation window and shakes his head no with widening eyes. Rachel applies portions of all the syringes in her case on the compound. Nothing has any effect. Cliff again shakes his head no. Rachel looks at the table and searches for an answer why this isn't working. She's as lost as the rest of them. She exits the clean room.

"Nothing?" Rachel inquires in clear frustration.

"You try everything?" Cliff asks.

"Yes," Rachel replies. She studies the monitor. Her wonderment over this new organism is rapidly being replaced with a more primitive emotion. She's used to being in control in the lab. She gets the feeling she isn't anymore. "What the hell are you?" She rhetorically spits. "It's not reacting to any of the agents. I don't understand," she continues.

Cliff is just as baffled. He types away on the console. The robotic arm picks up the compound sample tray, wheels across the room to the incinerator in the corner. Rachel shakes her head yes. If poisons won't kill it, fire surely will, she imagines. "Let's start at one hundred fifty degrees," she advises. Cliff types. The incinerator powers up, its burners spring to life giving off heat and light. The group studies the monitor again.

Jack and Beth are slack-jawed at the event unfolding before them. Jack can't help but to feel a sense of excitement, even though he has to temper himself. He's never seen Rachel get this upset at anything. That, more than the behavior of this material, is concerning to Jack. But his normal feeling of boredom has been replaced with a sort of Indiana Jones sense of adventure. At least for the moment.

As the group watches the monitor like hawks, searching for any kind of reaction out of the ZnMBe, it fails to comply. It just dances in the monitor, seeking out more to feed on. "One seventy five," Rachel commands. Cliff types. The fire in the incinerator gets brighter. The compound continues its defiance. Cliff types again to increase the temperature. The fire burns hotter. The compound stands its ground. Rachel's eyes begin to widen a bit. "Staph dies at one hundred seventy. Try two hundred," Rachel says. Cliff types. Jack approaches the window. He never considered the possibility they could have stumbled upon something dangerous. The thought sobers him up a bit. The compound continues to stand. It's clearly not Staph related.

"Take it up steadily in fifty-degree increments every few seconds," Rachel commands. Her goal to find containment protocol boundaries is being rivaled by the sheer will to beat this thing now. Cliff types.

"Two fifty," he announces. Rachel watches the monitor. The blood and water boil but the ZnMBe compound remains as if its plan is to beat the humans. Cliff types. "Three hundred," he announces. Jack looks at Rachel with a hint of concern. Rachel doesn't notice, her eyes fixated on the monitor. Cliff types again. "Three fifty," he says with disbelief. Rachel shakes her head.

"What the hell is this?" she rhetorically asks the universe.

"What can survive at this temperature?" Beth chimes in.

"Nothing," Rachel responds as if asking to explain the Red Sea parting. Cliff types again.

"Four Hundred," he says.

"Nothing," Rachel responds with clear concern in her voice. Cliff continues to type.

"Four fifty," he advises. Rachel and Jack's jaws slip open.

"Are you sure the temp is correct?" Rachel asks Cliff as if Cliff could have possibly made a mistake. Cliff shakes his head yes, but with the same level of concern. He would so very much like it to be wrong right now.

"Zinc melts at eight hundred," Jack interrupts the moment, more to provide a shred of hope than to show off his science knowledge.

"Five hundred," Cliff says softly.

The compound's dance begins to slow. Everyone's eyes widen at the hope this revelation brings. "Five fifty," Cliff says with more urgency. The ZnMBe compound separates from the zinc beryllium silicate and stops moving. You could hear a pin drop in the lab as everyone has stopped breathing, or at least that's how it sounds.

"Is it getting hot in here or is it me?" Cliff humorously breaks the silence. The group lets out a big breath with a chuckle. Rachel smiles at Cliff like he just pulled a prank on them. Cliff smiles back, thankful the event has ended. Jack and Beth chuckle and look at each other. Cliff fans himself and chuckles. "After that, I think we're ready for lunch," Cliff muses. Rachel agrees. "Let's do the live test this afternoon Jack," Cliff continues. Jack nods in agreement.

CHAPTER 7

The side door of the clean room opens on the far side of the room and Jason, clad in a protective suit, enters with a pair of cages. One has a small ape in it and the other a mouse. He sets the cart in the center of the room on an exam table and transfers the cages to it. He straps the cages down. Rachel enters the clean room and retrieves a case from the refrigerator. She approaches the animals. "The probes and micro cameras are in the hard case on the table," instructs Cliff. Rachel opens the case and removes the probe syringes. She carefully holds one of the large syringes and approaches the animals.

The micro camera probes were invented by Cliff at Barrister. They're one of his greatest achievements. He combined modern technology in a microscopic environment. The probes use a combination of heat signatures, sonar and HD digital video technology in a probe the size of a pinhead. The probe is injected into the bloodstream and as it circulates an image is generated by the activity around it. With this technology they have been able to document the movement of foreign bodies, viruses and even medications throughout the body and get a diagram from the inside how they affect the body, similar to the theory of the putting Dorothy in a tornado in the film Twister. The probe measures a variety of biological elements including blood pressure, density variations, blood thickness, platelet count, blood flow speeds and nutrient levels. The invention was enough to get Cliff's name in conversations for a Nobel.

She injects a cocktail into the ape which includes a dozen probes along with a solution containing the ZnMBe compound. The monitors in the lab spill mountains of data. Internal organ statistics, circulation metrics, and images which clearly separate the compound from the blood and organs. Vital signs scroll on a separate monitor.

Cliff gives Rachel a thumbs up that the injections successfully accomplished their task. Jack's eyes are glued to the monitors like he's watching a tense scene in a horror movie. Rachel approaches the mouse. She looks up at Cliff through the observation window. Cliff gives her the thumbs up. She injects the mouse. Monitors dance again. She bags the syringes and tosses them in a biohazard waste container. She gazes up at monitor feeds inside the clean room. So far there has been no indication of any activity or interaction from the compound.

Rachel is about to break her gaze when one monitor reveals a darkening hew which is indicative of circulation density change. Something is happening. The mouse squeals and writhes in its cage. Just then the ape starts twitching like it has a nervous tick. The probe monitor reveals the compound attacking blood cells. The blood cells surrender quickly and turn black like the compound cells. One turns to two. Two to four. Both animals twitch and convulse. Rachel switches attention back and forth between the monitors and the animals. Cliff, Beth and Jack appear slack-jawed in the lab. Jason's eyes bulge.

The mouse falls over and twitches. A drop of black colored goo drips from its nose. Rachel studies the reaction with a gaping jaw. Jack and Beth eye the action in horror from the lab. Suddenly the excitement of this find is giving way to a more sinister feeling. Beth covers her mouth at the mouse's horrific demise. Meanwhile, the ape writhes in pain. It flips itself onto its back and lets out a guttural scream of torment. Its chest rises and lowers several times in arrhythmic fashion before it slows and stops. The ape falls limp. Rachel shoots a look at Cliff in the lab. Cliff, mouth agape in horror, slowly shakes his head no to her. The monitors quiet down as if the faucet has been shut off. You could hear a pin drop. Nobody has words. They all stand in stunned silence for what feels like an eternity. Rachel sighs heavily to break the silence. She heads out of the chamber into the clean room where she changes in shock. She reenters the lab.

"What the hell happened?" demands Rachel.

"It just took them over and killed them in less than two minutes," Cliff slowly summarizes. The words leak from his mouth like a doctor delivering terminal family news. Rachel studies the monitors searching for a logical explanation that makes sense. She finds nothing but more questions.

"I've never seen anything like this before. Have you?" she confesses. Cliff stares at the dead animals in the clean room chamber. He eyeballs the monitors. He looks at Rachel with stunned shock in his eyes.

"No. Jack, you may have the scientific find of the century here," Cliff expresses. Jack smiles weakly, the irony of a major find that could end the world is not lost on him.

Not one person in the room wants to deal with the ramifications of this event. The possibilities are both hopeful and frightening simultaneously. The price to do great things is always high, but none of them expected this. However, this material provides a unique opportunity that Cliff can't ignore. Regardless of his personal disdain for the leaches at Hicks, they will not go away until he holds up his end of the funding bargain. But let's not get ahead of ourselves. Cliff knows he needs more information. And he needs some leverage. For that, he needs the people in this room. That starts with keeping their minds in the game.

"We need to celebrate," Cliff announces, breaking the tension. Rachel and Jack look at Cliff and break out of their nervous mood.

"Before we send our report to the CDC, I want to do the necropsy before they get cold," Rachel advises. Just the words Cliff needed to hear.

"We'll study the data and figure out what happened in there," responds Cliff. Rachel nods and heads for the lab exit.

"Good work Jack," Rachel says, patting Jack on the shoulder.

"Thanks," Jack smiles warmly.

Jack and Beth sit at the console and study the data tables. "Look at this," Beth announces. Cliff approaches them. The monitor broadcasting the internal feed from inside the animals is still relaying an image. Something is still moving.

"It's still feeding?" Cliff asks in wonder. Jack uses the playback controls for the camera to replay the last several seconds like using a DVR. He watches carefully and cross references the statistics data. "It consumed all the iron in the blood and then it multiplies simultaneously. The Beryllium accelerated the process so it would seem. It's shielding the bacteria from white blood cells here," Jack summates, pointing at a sequence on the monitor demonstrating a compound cell attacking red and white cells. He continues. "It's still working on tissue. But it slowed down. This is some hostile shit." Cliff listens intently.

"Less oxygenation maybe?" Cliff asks.

"Maybe," responds Jack without a better explanation.

"Upload the data to my server for analysis," requests Cliff.

"Already done," Jack replies confidently with a smile. Cliff smiles and pats Jack on the back. He hands him a Dixie cup of Champagne. Beth smiles warmly at Jack and he reciprocates. They toast together.

CHAPTER 8

The exam room of the Med Lab is a four hundred square foot glass enclosed clean room with six exam tables, a long countertop workstation and specimen refrigerator. This is Rachel's primary workspace. She conducts all of her exams here as well as necropsies, like the ones she's about to perform on the poor victims of the compound.

Rachel prepares a cart of surgical tools. The protective suit in this clean room is not as thick as the ones in the lab, so her gloves are surprisingly easy to work with. She rolls the cart over to the pair of exam tables which rest the dead mouse and ape. She stops the cart between the two tables and turns her attention to the ape. Both animals have been pre-prepped by Jason, so they are already pinned down to the surface. Rachel reaches above the table to the recorder controls and presses the red "Record" button.

"Dr. Rachel Barrister, Forensic Anthropologist at the Barrier Institute. Today is July 22nd, 2014. I'm conducting initial post mortem examination of two animal specimens, a mouse and an ape. Their deaths following the injection of a new bio-elemental compound ZnMBe. Death occurred within minutes of exposure. Necropsy to determine cause of death and potential human health hazards," she dictates. She probes the inside of the ape's mouth, retrieving a slimy black goo sample and places the swab in a vile and seals it. She places it on the tray. She collects another sample from the inside of the ear and nose.

Back in the lab, Jack and Beth pore over data from the monitor in front of them. Jack works out the details and points to the monitor. "The ZnMBe compound attacks the living cell. It consumes the iron and then infects the cell. That cell in turn looks for healthy cells to attack," Jack summarizes. Cliff looks at Jack with a hint of wonder mixed with fear. Out of the corner of her eye Beth spies the monitor broadcasting the mouse's internal probe. Something moved.

"What the hell?" she asks, clearly shaken. Jack and Cliff look at the monitor carefully. More movement. This is certainly disconcerting to all considering the mouse is dead.

"What is that?" Cliff asks confused.

"The micro camera inside the mouse. It's still transmitting," Jack replies, not realizing Cliff knows that but can't figure out why anything is moving in the mouse to begin with.

"The mouse died almost an hour ago," Beth chillingly reminds them. They all knew that, but hearing it out loud is like a real-life horror movie suddenly launching them into the nightmare. Chills run down their spine.

Back in Med Lab, Rachel lifts a syringe from the tray. "Extracting blood sample from the ape's heart," she announces to the listening recorder, which hovers above the room like a casual observer. She injects the syringe into the ape's chest and slowly pulls the plunger back, slowly filling the barrel. She places the full syringe on the tray gently. Movement catches her attention behind her. She turns to the mouse. You can hear a pin drop in here. Rachel stops breathing for a second as if trying not to give her position away to the boogie man. Nothing happens. She turns back to the ape and lifts another syringe.

Back in the lab, Cliff, Beth and Jack fixate on the mouse's micro camera monitor. They are trying to diagnose the logical explanation behind the movement they saw. Could it be a malfunction? Perhaps it's moving from displacing gases. Cliff checks the vital statistics monitor. No movement. This would indicate a malfunction in the camera possibly. "No vitals. It's definitely dead," Cliff concludes.

"But this is circulation," replies Jack with a hint of frustration in his voice. Suddenly the vital statistics monitor blinks and scrolls new data.

"Fuck me. I've got brain activity here," Cliff announces. Jack and Beth shoot a look in Cliff's direction with horrified eyes. Beth's jaw drops.

In Med Lab, Rachel circles the ape's table so she faces both tables from the head side. "Signs of advanced skin degradation and infection apparent. Rapid cell decline," she converses with her trusty recorder. The mouse twitches. Rachel's eyes bulge in that direction. She slowly plods toward the mouse. She's not breathing either, as if that will keep her presence more stealth like. But that's silly. The mouse is dead. Right? She's never been wrong about the death of a subject in all her years of science. Then why the fuck did it just move? she thinks to herself. The mouse twitches again. Rachel stops in her tracks. That was not the twitch of a nervous system glitch. It was like the leg moved. Trying to free itself. That is certainly not a twitch. Could she be wrong about it being dead after all? What seems like an eternity passes and no movement. Must have been a twitch. No other logical explanation makes sense. She steps toward it.

Cliff, Jack and Beth attempt to piece together the strange events that unfold before them in the lab. The brain activity in the mouse they're monitoring makes no sense. The mouse is dead. Isn't it? "These aren't normal brain wave patterns," Cliff informs them. On another monitor, the mouse's micro camera signals movement. Something is happening. Beth sees it and her eyes bulge.

"Jack?" she asks nervously. Jack whips around. Cliff looks up at them.

"What the hell?" Cliff rhetorically responds.

Rachel approaches the mouse slowly. The mouse twitches. This doesn't make her feel better. She leans in carefully, like approaching road kill. Her mask is slightly cloudy from her nervous breathing pattern. A leg breaks free from the pin holding it down, the pin still in the leg, looking like a nervous system reaction. Or at least that's what Rachel hopes. She stands to attention over the mouse. The leg moves around like it's trying to stand. This mouse is not dead. "What the fuck is going on?" Rachel spits. The mouse's eyes open, staring back at Rachel. They're red and white glazed orbs, nothing like the eyes it was born with. Rachel gasps and takes a step back.

Cliff continues to study the monitors. The vital stats monitor dances with bizarre brain activity. Jack shoots a look at Cliff and Beth. "They're not dead," he proclaims, realizing Rachel is alone with the animals in Med Lab. Cliff's eyes widen. Beth holds her hand on her mouth. Jack grabs the phone and dials.

Rachel slowly approaches the mouse again. Three remaining pins hold it in place for now. Rachel continues her report. "The mouse is apparently not dead after all. It's displaying rabies like symptoms. Eyes glossed over, red eye, bleeding from the mouth." The phone rings, interrupting her report. She jumps and sighs. She looks over at the phone and walks over to it. As her back turns from the animals, the ape's red and white glazed eyes creep open.

Jack holds the phone to his ear. "Come on, God damn it. Pick up," Jack blurts.

Rachel approaches the phone and picks up the receiver. "Hello?" she answers.

"It's Jack. Don't do anything. Something's wrong," Jack commands. The ape pries the right arm needle free. Then the left. Then the legs. It quietly pulls out the needles. It drops the needles to the floor. The noise grabs Rachel's attention. But she's afraid to look.

"What the?" Rachel inquires with a definite hint of fear.

"Rachel?" Jack calls from the phone receiver. Rachel slowly turns her head around. The ape stands on the table in an aggressive stance. Its bloody eyes stare at Rachel as if looking right through her. It gapes its jaw open wide. Rachel's eyes bulge with tears.

"Jack?" Rachel pleads weakly.

Jack shoots a look at Cliff with panic like he witnessed a shark attack. Cliff and Beth dart for the lab exit. "We're coming Rachel. Get the hell out of there!" Jack shouts and slams the phone down. He follows on Cliff and Beth's heels.

Rachel drops the receiver and slowly creeps toward the Med Lab exit. The ape stalks her with its eyes. Rachel spies a scalpel on a surgical tray and slowly reaches for it. On the other table, the mouse frees the last pin and wrestles with the needles until they fall to the tray. Rachel watches in horror. She just wants this nightmare to end. The mouse turns to her and glares at her through its glazed orbs like it knows her. Her eyes bulge and she stops momentarily. The mouse darts for her. She breaks for the door, which seems like miles away. The ape launches like a wild dog chasing a runner at Rachel. Rachel screams and trips over a chair.

Jason walks by Med Lab and sees the chaos happening inside. The soundproof room is even creepier with the visual horror taking place within. He approaches the door and stops. His eyes bulge with the sight of the grotesque homicidal ape lurking inside. Instead of entering and helping Rachel, he grabs the house phone on the wall next to the door. "Security to Med Lab. Something's happening. I don't know. Hurry. Fuck no I'm not going in there," Jason cowardly declares. He hangs the phone up.

Rachel wrestles the ape. It's unnaturally strong. It tosses Rachel across the room, slamming her into the table where the mouse was. She grimaces and shrieks in pain. The mouse retreats toward a wall vent. Rachel starts hyperventilating, fogging up her mask. She removes it in a panic. The ape tracks her and lunges. It wildly flails its arms and legs, scratching at her and biting her arm. Rachel screams in pain.

The door to Med Lab flings open and a security guard barges in with his weapon drawn. Cliff and Beth are right on his heels. Beth screams at the sight of Rachel on the floor in the corner with the ape draped over her like a wild animal. In the opposite corner, the mouse shoots through an open air vent and takes off for parts unknown. The ape turns from Rachel to address the guard. They have a momentary stare down. The guard lifts his weapon up to the ape with eyes open wide. He's never had to actually draw his gun before, let alone kill anything, and definitely not wild animals. The ape springs at him. He fires three quick shots. The ape hits the deck. The guard relaxes for a second and looks over at Rachel. The ape's eyes open wide again and it springs up looking pissed off. It growls violently at the guard. Jack bolts in and stops himself like he hit a wall. The guard shits his pants and unloads his clip at the ape. The final round clips the ape between the eyes just before it gets to him and it drops down again, motionless. The guard drops his clip and reloads waiting for the next attack. The ape stays down this time.

Cliff and Beth race over to the sprawled Rachel. Rachel shrieks and shakes when Cliff touches her. "It's me Rach," Cliff reassures her. Rachel recoils and takes a minute to get her bearings. Beth holds her hand tight. They help Rachel up into a sitting position. Cliff looks Rachel over and finds a tear in her sleeve above the wrist. "It broke the skin. Let's get her to Medical," Cliff appeals. Jack races out of the room and scrambles to find a wheelchair. He rushes it over to Rachel and they lift Rachel slowly into the chair. Jack wheels her out.

CHAPTER 9

The medical facilities at Barrister are set up like a clinic with two wings. The first wing is for minor medical issues and even small procedures and testing. The opposite wing is a secure wing that is used in case of quarantine, infectious disease or other needs with locked rooms with reinforced Plexiglas windows. This facility was built thanks to a Hicks Corporation grant. The fact the company hoped it would be used for weapons testing subjects was something Cliff never expected to happen. But in those days it was best not to look your gift horse in the mouth. The irony of the current situation is not lost on Cliff.

Cliff and Rachel met in the Biochemistry internship program at Stanford University in the fall of 1986. Cliff was a senior and Beth a freshman at the time and they were optimists in the purest sense of the word. In fact, that is what drew Rachel to Cliff in the first place. Before the lessons of life bent and then broke Cliff's ideology, he was well on his way to changing the world. They met at a rally where Cliff's mentor was lecturing on the needs of the mission fields of Africa and South America. Cliff was busted by Rachel "spicing up" the punch bowl to give it a little extra stress relief. It was a very cute moment that led to a three hour conversation about everything from ideology itself to the crazy ideas Cliff had in the areas of mixing biology with technology.Some of those inventions, including the micro bio-camera he even followed through with. Rachel listened for hours.

They went on their first date the next afternoon. In a world where it can be impossible to meet your soul mate, Rachel knew from the very first night. Not because she was caught up in the whims of romance. Not because he was an upper classman. Not because he was a dashing young man. In fact, he was the opposite. But when you meet someone whose life goals match your own and your paths are heading in the same direction that is something to take note of. The fact that his heart was filled with kindness, compassion and a desire to help humanity was the clincher for Rachel. She fell hard and deep for Cliff and him for her. They were married 3 months after Cliff graduated the following summer. Shortly after that, they received their first national attention from a paper Cliff published on elemental fusion efficiency. That was when Hicks entered his world. In those days Cliff was too naïve to see the dangers of getting into bed with big Pharma. It would take years for him to realize he was better off as a small fish in a big pond. When you're offered to have your dreams realized overnight, especially at such a young age, temptation is sometimes impossible to resist. Cliff saw only the good he could do in the world with all that money. And good he did to be sure. The cost of doing so much good was the variable left out of Cliff's equations. Would he still have made the same choices had he known? Nobody knows. Not even Cliff. But right about now none of that matters. They are where they are and there is no turning back.

Rachel lies on the bed in the regular patient room, pale as a ghost. Beth sits bedside, caressing her hand. A nurse applies antiseptic ointment to the scratch marks on her arm. She wears a surgical mask and gloves, which seems macabre considering it's Rachel Barrister in this bed. Cliff surveys the bite on her other forearm. The bite marks seep pus through red swollen tissue. "It's infected already," Rachel concludes. Cliff tries to hide the worry in his face. He can't help the sudden feeling they've opened Pandora's Box.

"Don't jump to conclusions," reassures Cliff.He's as much trying to convince himself than he is Rachel. He knows full well it's not only infected, but spreading fast and there isn't a damn thing he can do about it. Rachel smiles faintly through a furrowed brow. One of the many things she loves about this man is his never ending willingness to lie straight to her face to make her feel better. In a strange way, it does.

"Where's Jack?" Rachel inquires.

"Mixing you a wonderful cocktail," Cliff responds in a warm, reassuring tone. Cliff knows if there is one person he believes has the smarts to figure this out, it's Jack. Rachel and Beth smile faintly. The sense of death fills the room. Nobody has the nerve to speak its name, but like watching a ship sink without lifeboats, they know they need a miracle, and they are scientists. They don't deal in miracles. But it's amazing how quickly you'll be willing to turn to a higher power when hope seems lost. Cliff picks up a tweezers with his rubber glove and recovers a small tissue sample from the pussy mess at the bite site. Rachel cringes.

"Thank you," she says, hoping that something, anything will help. Cliff looks into Rachel's eyes.

"You're going to be fine," Cliff assures her. He smiles warmly at her and expresses his love for her in his eyes. They have been through everything together, and by damned they will get through this, Cliff thinks to himself. Rachel receives the message loud and clear. She smiles gratefully with tears running down her cheek.

Back in the lab clean room, Jack opens a plastic case in the freezer. He lays it gently on a table and opens it. He gently picks a bottle of Ciprofloxacin and inserts a syringe into it gently. He fills the syringe, removes it slowly and caps it. He repeats the process three times and places the syringes on a tray. He lifts the tray onto the two-way drawer and pushes it through. He exits the clean room, removes the suit and enters the lab and retrieves the tray carefully from the two-way drawer and places it on a cart. Jason types on a console behind him. "Kinda sucks what happened to Dr. Barrister," comments Jason. Jack stops and looks up at him.

"Yeah," Jack agrees, not wanting to engage him. Jason continues to type without looking up.

"Ciprofloxacin?" Jason inquires.

"Yeah," Jack responds again, wondering where this conversation is going.

"Hope for your sake it works," goads Jason.

"What?" Jack asks rhetorically with a touch of contempt.

"Just sayin. Hate to see your big discovery kill someone. Might ruin your chances with his daughter," Jason sarcastically scolds. Jason rises and locks eyes with Jack. That was a hell of a lot more than a shot across the bow. Jack ponders which action to take in response. In any other situation, Jason would be collecting his Chiclets from a bloody pool on the floor for taking such liberties. But Jack gets this is not going to help Rachel. Maybe he's growing up a bit. Maybe Jason's right. Who knows? But this is not the time nor the place for this. Jason smirks and exits the room. Jack follows him out with his eyes.

Cliff enters the room as Jason exits. "Hey," he calls to Jack. Jack breaks his gaze and looks at Cliff.

"Hey," he responds absently.

"Everything OK?" Cliff asks, noticing the distraction. Jack looks at Cliff and smiles. He picks the tray up and hands it to Cliff.

"Yeah. I'm gonna run an MRI on the ape and find out what the hell is going on," Jack advises. Cliff taps Jack on the shoulder, nods in approval and takes the tray.

"Keep me posted," Cliff requests. Jack heads out of the lab.

CHAPTER 10

The blood analysis lab is a relatively small fifteen foot square workroom with a work station counter, refrigerator, microscope station and blood chemistry analyzer. Jason enters the room and sits at the workstation. He loads a slide on to the microscope and writes notes on the pad next to him.

Jason started out as a promising young man. His SAT scores were in the top 5% nationally his senior year in high school. He had his pick of more than two dozen universities to study including Stanford and Ohio State. He gave all of that up in order to study at Waterston. Not because it was a top ten most prestigious private university. Not because he didn't want a mainstream education. He did it because he wanted to intern for Dr. Cliff Barrister. He worked hard his first two years in order to achieve the coveted position. He held it for over a year. He was the big dog on campus and everyone knew it. He knew it. They say that power corrupts. Perhaps that was his problem. Perhaps he grew a sense of narcissism achieving his goal so early in life. Whatever it was, something started him down a different path. He began showing up late for classes. His ideas in brain storming sessions became banal. For some reason, unknown to anyone including him, he simply started coasting. He was the man. He hadn't heard the old "what have you done for me lately?" cliché, or simply didn't think it applied to him. Either way, the grumbling started. And when Jackson Hart was offered a full scholarship to Waterston for his graduate studies, the writing was suddenly on the wall. And for someone so smart, the news that he was being replaced as Dr. Barrister's star intern came as a shock to Jason. More to the point, it hit him in his most vulnerable place. His ego.

Suddenly people stopped respecting him. They even laughed at him from time to time. Humble pie is tough to swallow for anyone. But for Jason it was especially bitter. He had no intention of taking it lying down. To add insult to injury, now Jack was moving in on Beth. Taking his internship with all the future opportunities it came with was bad enough. But this scrawny little punk was also stealing his girl. Not that Beth had betrothed herself to him, or even agreed to a date for that matter. But that was of little importance. The internship would have brought her affections with it. So now, it's on. Can't be hasty. Have to play the long game.

Then the perfect counter measure suddenly fell in his lap.ZnMBe. Jack's big discovery. The opportunity Jason needed. It presented huge problems to solve. And it doesn't hurt that it's infected Mrs. Barrister. It would be tragic if it kills her. But that is on Jack. In the aftermath, Jason can ride his white horse in and save the day amidst the smoldering ashes of Jack's demise. Oh what a grand day that will be. Soon. Very soon. In the meantime, he needs to solve the problem Jack's created. He needs his white horse.

He loads another slide on the microscope and records notes again. Nothing so far that will help. But he'll get there, he thinks deviously. He glances up from the microscope just as Lorna, the hot nurse from Medical strolls by. She flashes her long lashes at him with her little "ready for sex" smile she carries around with her like a razor. He smiles back as blood rushes to both of his heads. He imagines the next hook up and smiles ear to ear. He doesn't notice the zombie mouse which escaped Med Lab peek through the vent across the room. Nor did he eye the mouse lock its jaw on the vent and twist a hole big enough to crawl through.

Jack and Beth sit with an MRI tech in Medical. They study images from the zombie ape the guard put down earlier. The ape is strapped to the MRI machine and slides to and fro in the machine as images populate the tech's monitors. "The stats monitor still shows brain synapse, but no other vital signs," Jack reports like he's watching an episode of the Twilight Zone.

"It's coming up now,"the tech announces. The machine hums silently and images slide up the monitor. Beth studies the images carefully. She doesn't know what she's looking for but hopes she'll know when she sees it. Jack points at the screen image of the brain.

"What is that?" he asks the tech.

"The bullet severed the primary motor cortex," replies the tech.

"What's that?" Jack continues to inquire.

"Controls movement. Like the frontal lobe of the human brain," the tech educates. Jack looks at Beth like a light bulb just flicked on.

Jason puts head phones on and flips on music. The dry hum of noise bleeds over his ears and trickles away the silence of the room. The mouse stalks him. It carefully makes its way toward him with an intelligent purpose no mouse has ever had before. It knows what it's doing. It's doing it with malice. Just like a human being. Or something a little further up the food chain. Jason taps his foot to the beat of the music in his oblivious ears. The mouse stops for a brief moment to survey the situation. A tiny shadow under Jason's right pant leg reveals bare skin. Tough for the human eye to make out, but easy for this mouse's infected red orbs. It inches closer.

"I don't get it," Jack declares to himself. The thought is insane. But it's the only thing that makes any sense. The MRI tech's phone rings. He picks it up.

"Yes? I'll be right there," he says. He hangs up. "We good here?" the tech asks Jack as he rises from the console. Jack, still pondering the previous thought, breaks concentration to address the tech.

"Yeah, thanks," he responds passively. Beth, no longer even paying attention to the tech is still trying to wrap her brain around this.

"Circulation, brain synapse. But severing the primary motor cortex," she summarizes. Jack's head bobs in thought for a minute and then his eyes grow huge and he turns them toward Beth. "What?" she implores.

Jason peeps the eyehole on the microscope. He hums and taps rhythmically to the music droning in his ears. The mouse inches toward his ankle. Jason spins around in his chair. The mouse darts under the table. Jason rises and opens the fridge and grabs a soda and plops back down in his chair. The mouse finds the opening in his lower ankle again.

Jack peruses readouts. He studies the MRI screenshots. He gathers information to support his hypothesis. The tension gets to Beth. "What?" she inquires. Jack looks up at her and hesitates to speak. He knows this is going to sound nuts, and he wants to be right but never wanted to be more wrong at the same time. Now he even thinks he sounds nuts.

"You trust me?" he asks hesitantly. Beth, not expecting that response, feels a chill run through her fingers.

"Yes," she answers, not sure if she means it. But what choice does she have at the moment?

"Follow me. This thing ZnMBe fed on the ape from the inside and killed it. But it didn't stay dead. Or maybe it did, maybe this compound started controlling it. We have no vital signs other than brain synapse, but even those were not normal brain patterns. Rachel said it looked rabid. But severing the primary motor cortex dropped it. But according to this readout the compound didn't die," Jack summarizes.

"What are you saying?" Beth nervously asks. "

The ape is dead. But the bacteria isn't. Severing the primary motor cortex was like frying a motherboard on a computer. Without it, can't control its movement," Jack continues.Beth is still trying to piece the information together rationally. It's not working.

"The bacteria is controlling the dead ape," Beth parrots Jack.

"Exactly. Creates, I dunno, a zombie effect," concludes Jack, looking like he just opened a can of worms. Beth stares blankly at him.

Jason shifts in his seat and places his right foot flat right in front of the mouse. The mouse races by his leg and takes a small chunk of skin and flesh from Jason's ankle like a drive by shooting and races past him. Jason squeals and launches out of his seat, spilling the soda on the floor, missing the mouse by inches. He backs up and surveys the room to locate the cause of his pain. He looks under the table. Nothing. He moves the analyzer. Nothing. The mouse pauses quietly at the door to look back at Jason to celebrate its work. Satisfied, it bolts down the hall. Jason waits in silence. He sits slowly and pulls up his pant leg to scope the itching wound. The bite mark looks like a scalpel scrape with red pus filled blood leaking from it. "What the fuck?" Jason cries. He grabs the phone. "This is Jason in blood analysis. Something is loose in here and it just bit me. I don't know what it was. I didn't see it. Yes, I'm sure I was bit. I'm looking at it you asshole! I don't know, something big. Just send someone to check out the lab please. Right now!" Jason shouts, slamming the phone down. He lets his pant leg down and grimaces from the increasing discomfort.

CHAPTER 11

Beth Barrister was a senior in high school the first time she laid eyes on Jackson Hart. His name sounded funny to her, but in a sexy pop singer kind of way. Not that she would ever admit that to anyone. Thomas Jefferson High School always had its fair share of transfers in and out of its advanced studies program. Somehow Jack was not like most of the transfers that came and went. He clearly did not come from money. His dress and attitude told her that. Anyone who prefers shorts and t-shirts over khakis and pullovers was clearly not from a suitable education background. That was fine though Beth thought, because they need their occasional charity project from time to time. It makes everyone feel better about themselves.

One thing that annoyed Beth about young Jack, however, was his lack of social etiquette. He liked to invite himself on conversations, chiming in about things. He had an opinion about everything. He couldn't care less who knew it. Then there was the way he chewed his food at lunch. And the pranks he pulled. He was such a juvenile delinquent. Yes, it was quite obvious from the start. Beth Barrister really liked Jackson Hart.

"Zombie effect? Really?" Beth groans.

"I know it sounds nuts, but how else do you explain this?" Jack entreats. Beth stares at Jack for a moment, trying to find something, anything else that makes sense. But he has a point. As crazy as he sounds. Then her eyes widen as tears build. "What?"

Jack asks.# "It bit my mom," she breathes in horror. Jack's face flushes. He thinks for a moment.

"Come on," he blurts.

Cliff stands solemnly at Rachel's bedside. She's asleep. Cliff gazes at her for a long moment. Of all the adventures they've been on together, none of them has scared Cliff like this one. In all the years they've studied science, made discoveries and fought battles, none of them was ever like this. Even the cancer scare she had a few years ago wasn't like this. And Cliff never imagined anything could be that frightening. At least they knew what was attacking them and could courageously battle it. Like it or not, they have to do something. He will do whatever it takes. Cliff taps her hand gently. She awakens and smiles warmly at him. She's always loved waking up to that loving face gazing back at her.

"Hey," Cliff murmurs.

"Hey," she responds warmly.

"We're going to start you off on Ciprofloxacin," he advises. Rachel nods approval weakly through teary eyes. She hopes beyond hope it will help but her inner scientist has a bad feeling. Cliff carefully injects the medicine into her arm.

Jack and Beth enter the room. "Hey," Jack quietly announces. Cliff and Rachel look up at them. Jack nods at Cliff to come in the hall with him. Cliff exits the room with Jack. Beth sits at Rachel's bedside and holds her hand.

"What do you got?" Cliff inquires.

"We think the compound attacks the cells and consumes the iron in the blood and tissue. Then it takes the cell over and creates new compound cells, which in turn attack other healthy cells. Then once the body dies, it takes over the brain and circulates itself throughout the body to prevent rigor and keeps the brain alive to control motor function. However, evidence indicates trauma to the movement center of the brain prevents it from sending signals to the extremities. So when the ape was shot in the head it could no longer move," explains Jack.

"What happens when it runs out of healthy cells?" asks Cliff curiously. Jack looks at Rachel in the bed as the answer to that question is a horror he doesn't want to fathom.

"Look for new healthy cells elsewhere," Jack deduces.

"Rachel was bitten a while ago. The animals died in minutes. Maybe she's not infected," Cliff reaches. Sympathy washes over Jack like a warm blanket. He certainly understands the emotion, but it's just surreal coming from his mentor. But now is the time to be strong. No time for juvenile emotions.

"Humans are far more complex with more advanced immune systems," Jack assures Cliff. He's completely guessing, of course because he has no idea if that is even relevant. But it sounds reassuring, which is more important right now.

"I just gave her the Ciprofloxacin," Cliff advises, trying to gain his confidence back. Jack nods approval and touches Cliff's shoulder. They enter the room.

Cliff checks the monitor. "What?" Rachel inquires, having stalked their hallway powwow.

"Checking your vitals," Cliff responds, ignoring the real question.

"I feel it," Rachel responds.

"What?" Cliff asks.

"The compound. I feel it. It's getting worse," she advises. Cliff looks down at her.

"You can't know that," he assures her. He's caught in the purgatory of deep down knowing the truth and allowing himself to experience it. He knows denial is not the answer, but at the moment it feels like the only thing keeping him rational. But he also knows Rachel wouldn't say such a thing unless she was sure. He would do anything to save her. Right now, he's too close to be objective or have the focus to work the problem. He looks up at

Jack as if asking for his opinion. "The Ciprofloxacin isn't enough," Jack concludes. Beth tears up and looks away, fearing the worst. Cliff's face hardens.

"Keep looking," Cliff commands gently. A chill runs down Jack's spine as he realizes Cliff is counting on him to perform a miracle he's not convinced he can do. That's a lot to ask a young man. But he knows he will have to lay down any self-doubt if he's to have any chance of succeeding. He nods confidently at Cliff and heads for the exit.

"Jack," Rachel calls out. Jack turns to her. "Counter the Beryllium," Rachel surmises. Jack stares at her for a long second pondering the new information and calculating the new variable. His eyes light up.

"Beth, I need you," Jack insists. Beth looks up at Jack in surprise but with resistance. Cliff nods at Beth in approval for her to go with Jack. She doesn't want to leave her mother, but if it will help save her, of course she'll do whatever it takes. She rises and leaves the room with Jack.

CHAPTER 12

The Med Lab clinic is a small twenty foot by fifteen foot room with two exam tables, each with its own supply cart. The far wall hosts supply cabinets, lockers and a bathroom. Ceiling drawn curtains separate the two tables. It's designed for minor afflictions, cuts and sickness. It's also known as a hookup corner to horny employees.

Lorna is on duty today. This twenty three year old nurse is a page out of the classic candy striper stereotype. A blonde bombshell with legs for days with classic 36-24-36 measurements. You could assume she got through nursing school by fucking her way through, and you would be right. Having the perfect weapon to fight testosterone should be illegal. She's used sex as a weapon since the age of 12. She's basically fucked her way into the position she now holds at Barrister. Her sad truth is that she could've worked for everything she has because she is actually a very bright young woman and didn't need any assistance to pass her classes and is quite a talented nurse, in spite of her actions. But as another victim of being beautiful in a world that exploits such things, she was taught very young to use her body in any way it was beneficial for her to get what she wanted. She's not as shallow as that makes her seem, but her psyche is too scarred to know the difference now. She was hired to be the nurse at Barrister 6 months ago. She quickly realized who the alpha dog was among the up and coming minds at Barrister, and latched onto him with both hands, mouth and every orifice you can imagine.

Jason enters the room. Lorna turns from the supplies she's stocking and smiles warmly. "Hey," Jason simpers.

"What are you doing here?" Lorna responds in kind.

"Just wanted to see you," Jason replies. His aching ankle notwithstanding. Lorna smiles at him sensually.

"Really?" she says seductively. Jason sits on one of the exam tables.

"Yeah that and I need you to look at something," Jason requests. Lorna's eyebrows raise in a surprised, sarcastic tone.

"Now?" she questions seductively. Jason lifts up his pant leg. Lorna's brow furrows. "Oh," she says, dejected. The red pus filled bite stares up at her. She recoils. "What the fuck is that?" she demands.

"I dunno. Something bit me. Was hoping you could tell me what," Jason pleads. Lorna glares at him like he's teasing her. She puts on rubber gloves and scouts the wound.

"I have no idea. It looks infected," she concludes. Jason looks at the ceiling and sighs.

"Awesome," he retorts sarcastically.

"When's the last time you had a tetanus shot?" Lorna asks. Jason shrugs his shoulders.

Lorna proceeds to the supply cabinet and retrieves a syringe and a small bottle. She inserts the syringe and fills it. Jason's eyebrows raise hesitantly. Lorna rolls her eyes at him. "Don't be a pussy. It's just a tetanus shot. Lift up your sleeve," she demands. Jason complies. Lorna lines up the needle as Jason smiles at her. She glares at him as she pops the needle in his arm. He grimaces at the force she uses. Lorna removes the needle and drops it on a tray. She removes her gloves. "Don't be such a bitch," she playfully scorns. Jason smiles at her sensually, picking up on the signs of his horny nurse. She smiles back at him. She approaches him seductively. "You comin over tonight?" she sultrily asks. Jason nods yes without breaking eye contact, his mouth slightly agape as his arousal takes shape on his face. She slides her hand slowly up his leg, gently squeezing his upper thigh as his crotch grows in front of her, making her blood pressure rise. Her hand probes his six-pack abs and up his chest as his hands find their way to the middle of her back, stroking gently. She purrs softly. She puts her hands over his head and he pulls her gently to him. He smiles. She gazes at his lips and lightly bites her own. Her elevated breathing pattern obvious, she inches toward his mouth. He readies for the sweet taste of her lips and tongue. She teasingly sticks her tongue out and touches his upper lip with it. No longer having the capacity for teasing, he grips her back strongly, edging the last two inches between their mouths and gently sucks on her tongue. She moans with pleasure as he reaches down to her ass and caresses it. Lorna drops her hand to his belt and unbuckles it. They both moan in pleasure as they explore each other's tongues. Jason's member throbs and he comes up for air, gasping for breath. She takes his member in her hand and he moans. He leans back on the table as she goes down on him. He moans loudly. She puts her finger in his mouth and he sucks it gently. He coughs. She continues to bobble on his dick. He grabs her head and brings it to his face and puts his tongue deep in her mouth as she rubs his cock with her hips. She moans in pleasure. He convulses. She notices the break in concentration and removes her tongue from his mouth and looks at him. He looks at her. He kisses her again. She moans. His eyes bulge and he pulls out of her mouth. She opens her eyes to see what he's doing and he looks right at her and launches a green chunky vomit spray right in her mouth and all over her face. She immediately recoils in horror and screams.

She looks at Jason in utter horror and then convulses and turns and races for the bathroom. She dives at the toilet just in time for her own bile filled spray to cake the commode. She cries hysterically as she heaves again and again. The waves finally subside and she sits on the floor next to the toilet for a minute. Jason reaches out a towel to her. She violently swipes his hand away. She flushes the toilet violently and stands at the sink.

Lorna's vomit snakes its way through the sewer pipes until it reaches the sewer below. It splashes near a group of curious rats. They trot by and sniff around the slimy mess.

"Get the fuck out!" Lorna shouts at Jason. She slugs past him to a locker. She opens it and removes her vomit stained blouse.

"Lorna," Jason pleads. Lorna sighs loudly and rolls her eyes. She stops for a second and looks at Jason.

"Just go. Go see your doctor. You'll be fine," she advises. She gets that this wasn't his fault, but she's pissed as fuck anyway. Jason goes to the sink and washes the vomit off his face and slinks past Lorna out of Medical. She follows him out with hostile eyes.

CHAPTER 13

Back in the lab, Beth and Jack sit at a console. Jack types a mile a minute. "What are we looking for?" Beth entreats.

"The Beryllium is shielding the bacteria. Preventing us from fighting it," Jack replies.

"Right? So?" Beth asks again.

"So we can't just fight the compound. We also have to treat the Beryllium, which can kill her even if we could get to the compound. Any remedy is useless without removing the Beryllium from the equation," Jack summarizes. Beth thinks for a long minute.

"So we need a corticosteroid. We have Prednisone," she advises. Jack looks up and smiles at her.

"Let's prepare a cocktail of the Ciprofloxacin and Prednisone," he says.

"But we don't know what that will do to her," Beth warns.

"We know what will happen if we don't," replies Jack solemnly. Beth stares at Jack for a second as the revelation of Rachel's certain death hovers over her like a dark cloud. It's not fair. None of this is fair. Rachel has always tried to help people. Beth ponders these dark thoughts as she strolls over to the medicine cabinet.

Logan waits impatiently at the reception desk at the front entrance of the institute. He is clearly agitated and has no intention of being passed off today. It's not that he takes Cliff's avoidance tactics personally. He's a professional after all, and doesn't subscribe to such child's play. It's rather that he has powerful forces who expect results from him. He can't deliver those results from Barrister without Cliff. So here he waits.

Cliff enters the wing. "Cliff," Logan calls out. Cliff stops in his tracks as if caught with his hand in the cookie jar. But now is not the time to give Logan a guided tour. Not yet. They aren't ready.

"Logan. I don't have an appointment on my schedule," Cliff responds.

"I don't need one. Do I?" Logan inquires, as if a foregone conclusion he was welcome whenever he felt like being there. Cliff scratches his head and looks up at Logan. The liberties Logan enjoys taking with him feel more like a dick measuring contest to Cliff. As much as he loves a good power struggle, he has bigger fish to fry.

"What can I do for you?" Cliff asks as if he doesn't already know the answer.

"Need an update," Logan answers matter of fact.

"On?" Cliff stalls. Of course he knows what the man wants. He always wants the same damn thing. He's like a dog with a bone. Logan, sensing the stall tactic, simply raises his eyebrows through a wry smile and shrugs his shoulders. Cliff sighs. "I'm working on it," he replies coldly.

"I need more," Logan persists. It's not the first time they've danced this number either, but Logan does tire of it.

"That's all I have right now," Cliff counters.

"You think I can go back with "working on it"?" Logan warns. He doesn't want to threaten Cliff, but he's not taking the subtle direction. So a more direct approach is needed. Cliff, receiving the message, and the pressure that goes with it, stares into Logan's eyes.

"I just need time," Cliff requests with a hint of humility in his voice.

"That's a luxury neither of us have," Logan replies, keeping the pressure on. Cliff knows he can't run or hide from this. But if he tells Logan about ZnMBe now, it could blow up in both their faces.

"I'll get you something today. I'm just dealing with something right now. OK?" Cliff pleads.

"I'll wait," Logan replies, not sure whether Cliff is actually being honest or has developed new stall tactics. Either way, he's not leaving until he has something to take with him. Cliff glares at Logan. Logan reciprocates. Cliff's face softens a little. He nods and smiles and heads for the opposite wing. Logan, not trusting a word that comes out of his mouth, watches him leave. Today he will watch him like a hawk.

Jason enters the break room. It's a relatively quaint fifteen foot square space outfitted with a pair of couches, another pair of chairs and a mini-fridge. The room is empty. Jason counts his blessings as he staggers up to one of the couches and plops down on it. He feels drained like he felt the last time he had the flu bad. Why he feels like that now, he doesn't know. Flu doesn't just hit you out of nowhere. But he's not feeling well at all. He looks up at the fluorescent light above and it hurts his eyes. He grimaces. He lies down on the couch and turns his back to the center of the room. Maybe he'll feel better after a nap.

Jack and Beth stand next to Rachel's bed. Her swollen eyes inch open through her pale complexion. She's clearly on death's door. Jack prepares a syringe. Cliff enters the room and sees them. His eyes brighten a bit at the hope that Jack found a solution. "We got something," Jack advises. Cliff's eyes widen with hope.

"What?" he asks eagerly.

"We can't fight the compound without addressing the Beryllium. It's killing her as much as the bacteria," summarizes Jack.

"So we're using Prednisone to counter the Beryllium," Beth continues. Cliff studies Beth's face for a moment, letting the information settle and she nods approval.

"What will that do to her?" Cliff inquires. Jack stops for a moment.

"Don't know. But what choice do we have at this point?" Jack counters. Cliff stares at the syringe like it's the worse decision he's ever been asked to make. He has no idea how they even got to this point. He puts on rubber gloves and holds out his hand. Jack slowly places the syringe in his hand and proceeds to the end of the bed.

Cliff holds the syringe for a long moment. How he wishes there were someone who could tell him the right thing to do to save Rachel's life. All his knowledge and training, all the lives he's saved, all of his contributions to humanity.None of that will save the love of his life. All their hopes pinned on a solution of poisons that would likely kill a normal person. The insanity claws at Cliff's mind. He takes Rachel's hand. "You ready?" he asks weakly. Rachel smiles at him as the tears stream down her cheeks. She nods, being unable to speak the words. She knows full well what happens if this doesn't work. She always thought she'd grow old with Cliff. Tomorrow is never guaranteed for anyone, but she never believed the end would come like this. She's not ready. But here we are.

Beth and Jack watch the monitors closely. The compound races through her body killing the last of the remaining healthy cells she has left like a wave of locusts consuming everything in their path. Her vital signs slow to dangerous levels on another monitor. Rachel squeezes Cliff's hand. If this is the end at least she will be with the love of her life. She has that solace at least.

Cliff injects the solution into Rachel's arm. He holds her hand and looks deep into her eyes. He sees the best moments of their marriage flash before his eyes. Through everything they've been through, he's never loved her so much as he does right now. Jack and Beth continue to monitor the data. The micro camera picks up the solution meeting an infected cell. The bacteria portion writhes. The Beryllium separates from the cell. Her pulse rate increases. Cliff smiles. It's working. He looks at Jack. Jack smiles back like watching the end of a tense movie.

Just as Jack looks back at the monitor a group of infected cells surround the solution that was attacking the other infected cell. Jack's smile immediately disappears. More infected cells attack. The solution dissipates and the infected cells march on. Rachel's breathing labors as if the compound is punishing her for the intrusion. Cliff looks at Jack in desperation. "We're on the right track. We just need time to get the solution right," Jack assures Cliff.

"Get on it," Cliff commands. They all know they're running out of time. They have no time to waste.

Just as Jack heads out of the room, an alarm squeals from the monitor over Rachel's bed. Her vitals are crashing. Jack whips around in horror. Rachel convulses violently. Cliff slams the emergency button on the wall. "Code blue! Get in here!!" Cliff screams. A nurse rushes into the room with a crash cart. Beth and Jack leap out of the way. Beth covers her mouth. Cliff opens Rachel's gown, preparing for defibrillation. Rachel convulses again. Jack grabs Beth, who is sobbing. She holds Jack tight and turns her face away from the horror of watching her mother dying.

The vitals monitor suddenly falls quiet. Rachel's body relaxes and slumps. Cliff breathes hard, trying to find a way to alter this outcome. His eyes fill with tears. His face suddenly hardens. He grabs the defibrillator paddles. The nurse widens the gown opening. Cliff charges the paddles and places them on Rachel's chest. Rachel's body jumps but no change in the vitals monitor. Cliff resets at a higher voltage. He paddles her again. No change. Cliff battles shaky hands to up the voltage a third time. Nothing. God damn it, why isn't this working? he roars in his mind. He drops the paddles and begins CPR. The nurse pumps oxygen into Rachel's mouth at regular intervals. Cliff continues to pump. Flatline. Tears stream down Cliff's cheek. Jack looks at Cliff somberly.

Over two minutes have passed. Cliff tirelessly continues CPR. His brow sweats. Jack slowly approaches Cliff and touches his arm. Cliff ignores him. Jack touches him again. Cliff shrugs him off. The nurse stops her oxygen hand pump and steps back from the bed. It's no longer about trying to save Rachel. Now they need to bring Cliff back. The tragedy of losing the love of your life is one that not many can comprehend. It'snot something that can be explained. It can only be understood through the experience of tragedy. One that no human should have to endure. At least not like this. "Daddy," Beth pleads through tearful sobs. She approaches him and puts her arm around his waist. Cliff feels the warmth of his daughter's love through her tender touch and stops pumping Rachel's chest. He lets out a light sob of his own. The nurse closes Rachel's gown. Cliff turns and embraces Beth. They stand and cry in each other's arms.

Jack eyes the vitals monitor. The heart is not beating, but it's not completely flat-lined either. The smallest of arrhythmia identifies some kind of activity through the cardiovascular system. Jack inspects Rachel's eyes. Cliff turns to address him. Rachel's eyes begin to change color. They are reddening ever so slowly. "Cliff," Jack calls. Cliff looks. "We need to secure her," Jack continues.

"What?" Cliff replies, not catching up to the logic.

"The animals," Jack reminds Cliff. It clicks that whatever killed the animals has killed Rachel. And like the animals, it's not done yet.Shit is getting real. Cliff glares at Jack. His rage over this compound grows worse by the minute. Beth's jaw drops.

Cliff checks the vitals monitor. "Hold on a minute," he spouts. He races to the corner of the room where a case rests on a table. He opens it and removes a syringe and grabs his phone. He goes back to Rachel's bedside. He injects the syringe into Rachel's arm. "Micro camera. Let's have a look," Cliff says. He launches an app on his phone and logs in. He selects the serial number for the camera he just injected into Rachel's arm. An image immediately reveals circulation in Rachel's body. The compound is feeding off healthy cells in tissue. Cliff shoots a look at Jack. "Observation Room B. It's Plexiglas and we can monitor her from there," Cliff commands with a renewed sense of purpose. Jack isn't following what has him in this condition, but he knows they need to secure Rachel quickly. Jack grabs a strap from under the bed and he and Cliff strap Rachel down. Everybody leaves the room as Cliff and Jack race the gurney toward the secure wing. Cliff has a plan.

CHAPTER 14

Observation Room B is a twelve by twelve foot square room equipped with a crash cart, hospital style plugs for power, oxygen and the like and several monitors. It is normally used for test subjects in drug trials or addicts undergoing treatment. They never dreamed it would be used for this.

Cliff and Jack roll Rachel into the room and connect the monitors. Jack checks Rachel's eyes. They are glossed over and deep red. They stare at nothing. "It's started," Jack states. Brainwaves dance in a creepy pattern on the monitor. Cliff ties down all of Rachel's limbs. Both stand at the foot of her bed. They stare at her in a surreal desperation that this new discovery could destroy everything they love. For the first time Jack experiences the sting of responsibility of bringing this nightmare into their lives. In reality, none of this is his fault. But this family took him in as their own, or at least made him feel that way, and he feels a responsibility to make it right. The only question is how.

"Are you sure the bacteria is keeping her brain alive?" Cliff asks randomly. Jack looks at Cliff, wondering where he's going with this.

"Yes," he replies. Cliff looks at Jack with determination in his eyes. But not the determination of his mentor. The determination of a desperate man.

"Then maybe we have time," Cliff surmises. Jack's eyes widen. "If there's any chance, we have to try," Cliff continues. It suddenly hits Jack. Cliff hasn't given up on trying to save Rachel. He can't blame him. And who says they can't? Nobody has ever seen this material before. If there is a chance, he's right. They have to try.

Jack nods and places his hand on Cliff's shoulder. Rachel's eyes open and she raises her head. But it's not Rachel. Not anymore. At least not the Rachel they know and love. She struggles with the restraints as she glares at both Jack and Cliff like they're on the menu. Jack and Cliff share a look. "Hurry," Cliff pleads. Jack exits.

Cliff realizes there is nothing he can do for Rachel right now. But he may be able to help Jack. He can collect the research from his office. Any new information could possibly help. He exits the room and snakes through the hallways to the Admin wing to his office.

He enters his office. Logan is perched at Cliff's desk typing on his computer. "What are you doing?" Cliff interrogates. Logan picked a fuck all day to get nosey.

"Catching up," Logan retorts. Cliff picked a fuck all day to get secretive. The sport of their sparring has become rather entertaining over the past few years but this is different. This could get ugly.

"I told you I'd have something for you today," Cliff quips.

"I got tired of waiting," Logan shoots back. Logan knows he's holding back and he's not going to have any of it.

"It's not ready yet. We don't know what it is yet," Cliff concedes. He's taking a big risk, hoping to get Logan on his intellectual side. Not today though.

"No matter," Logan fires back.

"I have something to deal with. I need the day," Cliff pleads.

Logan tires of Cliff's stalling. He looks out the window and sighs as he prepares to lay it on the line for Cliff. "You ever read Edmund Burke?" Logan asks passively. Cliff feels it coming like that moment your stomach contracts itself right before you vomit. He sighs. Logan continues, "Eighteenth century political theorist and Irish member of English Parliament. A brilliant man. He supported the American War of Independence from England. Yet he's more remembered for coining the phrase "don't bite the hand that feeds you"."

"It killed Rachel," Cliff reveals. He didn't want to have to go there, but Logan left him no choice. He needs time to save her if he can. And Logan painted him into a corner. But if this revelation buys him enough time to save Rachel before Hicks blows it all up, it's worth it.

Logan turns back to Cliff and studies his face for honesty. He would never have expected that string of words to escape his lips unless he was desperate or it was true. Maybe it's both. Logan takes a second to process the information. He concludes Cliff wouldn't bring the love of his life into the conversation unless it was true. He sits on the couch. "I'm sorry. You have until the end of the day," Logan agrees. Of course, he still doesn't have a clue what they're dealing with. And Cliff is thankful for that. But at least he got what he needed.

Rats with red glazed orbs snake their way through the sewer beneath the institute. Like a battalion of mini soldiers marching in formation, they turn corner after corner. Other rats, mice and even insects avoid them. There is something wrong with these animals. A noise from around the next corner catches the rat's attention and they peek carefully. A middle-aged homeless man snores loudly atop his box bed. The rats glance at one another.

Back in Cliff's office, Logan waits patiently for word sitting on the sofa. His phone beeps an announcement that he's received a new text. He pulls the phone from his pocket. He launches the message. "FROM NORRIS: Update?" reads the message. Logan types his response "Have a potentially lethal bio-weapon, waiting for files". The response from Norris: "Need to brief SECDEF soon". Logan responds: "Copy. I'll move it along". Even though Logan may not agree with everything that happens in his job, he is loyal to a fault and a good foot soldier. But he wasn't lying to Cliff. Shit really does roll downhill. He knows Cliff needs time, but that is a luxury neither of them have any more. Logan stands and exits the office.

In the lab, Jack types hard on a computer console while Beth sits nearby on a chair. Her shrunken appearance and blank stare catch Jack's attention. Monitors flash images and information and Jack takes notes. He looks at Beth again. He can't concentrate on his work. She's hurting and he needs to address that now. He's not used to this feeling. He actually loves her. He doesn't really know her that well, but it doesn't matter. She may not love him back. But he loves her. And right now, she needs him.

He rises and strolls to her and sits next to her. "Hey," he says consolingly.

"Hey," she replies in a broken voice.

"How are you holding up?" he inquires gently.

"Not well," she replies weakly. Jack hasn't been in this position. He wants to make her feel better. He just doesn't know how.

"We've not given up on her," he assures her. Beth shoots Jack a WTF look.

"Jack. My mom is dead. My dad can't handle it. It's not going to be alright. It's never going to be alright again. I know you want to appease my dad. But at least I haven't lost my grip on reality. Fuck!"she exclaims. Jack looks at her in shame. Stupid move he thinks to himself.

"You're right. I'm sorry," Jack murmurs.

He stands to go back to the console. He feels like shit for making it worse instead of better. Beth grabs his hand as he turns away. He turns back. She leads him to sit back down. He does. She leans and kisses him warmly. Jack is taken aback by this sudden show of affection. But it is more than welcome. "What's that for?" he asks.

"I never thanked you," she replies warmly. Jack looks at her trying to recall something he did that she would be that thankful for but comes up empty. He looks into her eyes. He's trying to hide his feelings, but he sucks at that too. "For helping me with my research paper in Mr. Morgan's class," she states with a warm smile. She gets Jack isn't the most experienced person at consoling someone. But he is trying. He is reaching out to her. And she loves that. She loves Jack. She doesn't like it one bit. But she does. And right now, when the world is going to complete shit, it's alright to admit that. If only to herself. Jack takes a moment to recall the memory she's talking about and smiles.

"Which time?" he responds with a little sarcasm. A lighter mood is welcome right now. Beth smiles.

"You were always the smartest kid in class. I hated that," she lies. That was one of his most endearing qualities. But never tell that to a boy. It goes straight to their head.

"Why?" he asks.

"Because in spite of my obvious signals, you never asked me out," she proclaims. Jack takes a second to process this statement. She's telling him she had feelings for him too. He wasted a golden opportunity and didn't even know it.

"What?" Jack replies in horror.

"For someone so smart, you can be pretty stupid," she continues. Jack's face flushes with embarrassment. He really needs to work on his interpersonal skills he thinks to himself. But back to the matter at hand.

"What signals?" he asks inquisitively.

"I asked you to tutor me," she reveals. Jack isn't there yet.

"So?" he asks.

"At my house," Beth replies with widening eyes, hoping Jack will comprehend the flirtatious nature with which she tried to express her feelings for him. Jack sits up, connecting the dots in his mind. "On the weekends," Beth continues, walking him through the beats where she all but asked him out herself. Jack is finally connecting the dots. He feels even more stupid than before. He stares at Beth with wide eyes.

"Unbelievable." He scolds himself for being so stupid.

Beth laughs. "My mom made you food," Beth pours it on. Jack laughs.

"She made awesome snacks." Conceding his stupidity. The thought grabs Beth like she walked into a wall. Her face turns sad in an instant.

"I wanna see her," she breathes. Jack stops laughing and looks at her. She no longer looks like the mom Beth remembers. It's not a pretty picture.

"I'm not sure that's a good idea," Jack pleads. Beth looks at Jack with begging in her eyes. She searches for closure. Jack is not certain she will find it. But he can't fault her for wanting some. He doesn't want her to have to go through that. But she is anyway. Jack gets up and nods to her. He extends his hand. Beth takes it and stands. Jack softly cups Beth's face in his hands. He gently kisses her. She wraps her hands around his. "Alright," Jack breathes.

CHAPTER 15

The animal holding facility at Barrister is a twenty five by thirty foot rectangular room enclosed with Plexiglas exterior windows and contains rows of cages and Plexiglas pens built in the walls and stacked in the aisles. There are apes, mice, rats, dogs and rabbits housed here. The noise is like that of a pet store. But there is no happy ending for these test animals.

The red orb eyed mouse creeps in through a vent shaft. It peeks into the room. The noise level increases as the animals all sense its presence.

Jack and Beth approach Observation Room B. Beth spies Rachel through the Plexiglas as they enter the room. Rachel now more resembles someone in need of an exorcism than her mother. Her corpse has turned green/black and she writhes against her restraints like a wild animal. Beth covers her mouth and tears up. Rachel is not even a shell of her former self. Cliff enters the room with a thermos in his hand. "I asked you not to bring her here," Cliff bemoans.

"I wanted to come.I'm OK," Beth expresses. Cliff studies Beth for a moment, unable to figure out why anyone would want to be in this room. The grotesque form her mother suffers in right now won't help anyone. But he won't deny her if that's what she wants.

"Where are we on a solution Jack?" Cliff inquires, more to change the subject than to expect a good answer.

"Working on it," Jack replies.

"Work faster. Hicks wants the compound and I can't get rid of Logan," Cliff demands. Jack nods compliance. Beth looks at the thermos Cliff has in his hands.

"What's that?" she asks curiously.

"You don't want to know," Cliff advises. Jack looks at Cliff and a chill runs down his spine as he thinks he knows exactly what's in that thermos. Jack can't help but to wonder if this whole situation is just too much for Cliff. Maybe he is breaking psychologically.

Cliff sits bedside and removes the lid from the thermos. He pours a sample of its red payload into a cup. Beth's eyes widen. "Oh my God," she proclaims.

"What are you doing?" demands Jack.

"Buying you time. The compound needs healthy blood to feed. It's feeding on her tissue right now. Stands to reason if I give it fresher blood it will leave her tissue alone, giving you time to find a way to kill it," Cliff summarizes. As insane as that sounds, Jack also sees the logic in it. Some moments Jack wishes he didn't suddenly know as much about the real world. Life was so much simpler when he could sleep late and play pranks. He's a long way from home in that regard now. People's lives are at stake. Counting on him. That thought would sober any drunk.

"Dad," Beth pleads. Cliff looks at Beth.

"What?" he answers.

"Don't," she continues. Cliff realizes he looks nuts. And he realizes his loving daughter is trying to reel him back to reality. This must be hell for Beth he thinks. But when they solve the problem she'll see. Just need to wait until they do.

Jack's brow furrows. "Where did you get that?" Jack asks. Cliff looks at him confused. Jack points to the thermos. He is clearly referring to the "fresher blood", Cliff looks away and sighs. Then he turns back and glares at Jack. Jack does the math. "The animals," Jack concludes.

"What?" Beth asks horrified.

"Don't judge," Cliff retorts. "I am trying to save your mother. Do you understand that? If killing an animal helps me save her, what would you do?" Cliff defends himself.

The room is silent for a moment as the horror and logic of Cliff's words resonate in Beth and Jack's ears. They may not like it but the man has a point. Who wouldn't sacrifice an animal to save a loved one? Jack ponders for a moment and has an epiphany. His eyes light up and he raises an index finger. Cliff stands and Beth turns to him.

"Misdirection. That's it," Jack exclaims. Cliff looks confused. "Give it to her in small but steady doses. We'll be back in twenty minutes," Jack continues. Beth looks at Jack sideways like he's losing it too.

"What are you thinking?" Cliff interrupts.

"We're running out of options and time. Going to test a theory," Jack proclaims. Jack looks at Beth. "Come on," he requests. She has no idea what is going on with these two. She feels like she's in the middle of a psychotic episode. But they believe in what they're doing. And if this insane idea brings her mother back, that is all she cares about at this moment. She exits the room with Jack.

Back in the break room, Jason lies on his side sleeping. His raspy breathing pattern becomes erratic. It slows. Slower and slower. It finally stops. Jason lays motionless. His change has begun.

Cliff uses a dropper to trickle drops of animal blood into Rachel's blackened mouth. Rachel greedily accepts each drop. Wanting more. She gives her full attention to Cliff. Just one wrong move and he can give her a whole fresh source of nourishment. But for now, she takes the trickle.

Logan enters the room. His mouth agape, he forgets to breathe for a second. Cliff spies him out of the corner of his eye. "Oh my God, is that Rachel?" Logan gasps. Cliff glares at him. "I thought you said she was dead," Logan continues. Cliff sighs heavily like someone busted with their hand in the cookie jar.

"She is," he replies defiantly. That statement slams Logan like a punch in the face. How can she be dead? Logan studies Cliff and looks at Rachel. He's as excited as he is horrified. The contrasting emotions burn a hole in his stomach.

"Why didn't you tell me about this?" Logan demands. Cliff stares back at Logan in disbelief. He would never believe Cliff even if he told him. Or the more scary thought, maybe he would. Either way, Logan is not concerned with saving Rachel.

"Let me take her back to Hicks. Maybe we can help," Logan lies. Cliff is not buying it.

"No," Cliff retorts. Logan stands for a moment pondering his next move.

"What are you going to do?" Logan asks, treading lightly.

"Reverse the process and then tell the CDC," replies Cliff. Logan again ponders the options before him. The last thing he wants is to turn this information to the CDC. And as much as he likes Cliff, this is business. He has to take control of this.

"That won't be necessary," Logan announces.

"What are you talking about?" Cliff inquires, his tone turning hostile. It's time for Logan to tell him how it is.

"You've done well Doctor. Get the files ready. We'll transport her tonight," Logan commands. Cliff begins to see the inevitable writing on the wall. What he feared most is happening right now.

"You can't do that. We have to report this," Cliff advises, playing the ethical long game. Ironically Cliff left ethics in his rear view a while ago. Logan gets it. And somehow he knew it would eventually come to this which is why he kept ammo in his back pocket.

"While we're in the reporting mood, we should call the IRS and the Department of Justice," Logan warns.

"What?" Cliff exasperates, not ready for the ultimatum. Logan releases the second barrel.

"Embezzling grant money is a crime," Logan accuses. Cliff sighs in anger. "I told you to seek help for your gambling problem," Logan continues, keeping rhetorical pressure on Cliff's throat. Cliff glares at Logan.

"What do you want?" Cliff asks angrily. Logan, satisfied that Cliff is finally on the same page, smiles.

"You have two hours," Logan insists. Logan exits the room. Cliff stands catatonic for a moment. He can't believe this is happening. He still thinks he can save her. Maybe he is crazy. Maybe this whole experience has only proven Cliff to be the fraud he was always afraid he was. He now has two hours to find out.

CHAPTER 16

Jack types feverishly on a console in the lab. The ape that attacked Rachel lies motionless on a table in the clean room. Beth stands next to it in her protective suit. She carefully injects the ape with a syringe containing the latest trial cocktail they're working on to save Rachel. The monitors indicate the compound defiantly resisting the latest solution. Beth looks at Jack and shrugs her shoulders to indicate she has no idea why it's not working. Jack pounds the counter in frustration.

"That's at least fifty combinations! What are we missing?" he complains.

"Maybe it's invincible," Beth replies, not meaning to sound as sarcastic as it was.

"Nothing's invincible," Jack bellows.

Beth stares at the ape for a long moment and then her eyes widen as she looks at Jack. "Counter the Beryllium," she says revelatory. Jack looks up at her.

"What?" he inquires.

"That's what mom said. Counter," Beth repeats. The synapses in Jack's brain calculate this information for a moment. He stares at Beth. His eyes widen. He plops down at the console and types. Beth approaches the safety glass and tries to see what Jack's doing.

"What are you doing?" she asks.

"History lesson," pipes Jack. Jack suddenly realizes they have been approaching this all wrong. Sometimes answers are found by looking back, in history, instead of forward. He continues to type while Beth watches on in hope.

"Got it. January, 1952. Aurintricarboxylic acid. Tested positively in reversing Beryllium poisoning," Jack exclaims triumphantly. Beth ponders for a minute.

"Ammonium salt," she concludes. Jack looks up at her and smiles.

"Yes! Mix that with the Prednisone and add saline, then add Ciprofloxacin," he instructs. Beth nods yes and smiles. She turns back toward the fridge and pulls two containers out with syringes. She lays out all of the materials on the workbench. She collects the elements in a beaker and swirls it together. She carefully pours the contents of the new solution into a syringe jar and seals it. She fills four syringes with the new solution.

"You sure this will work?" Beth asks Jack, looking up at him.

"Nope. But we have no time," Jack replies hopefully. Beth nods that she understands.

"Ready," she announces.

"Inject the ape," Jack requests.

Beth carefully takes a syringe and injects it into the ape. The compound ignores the solution in the monitor. The solution attacks a compound cell. They struggle as if in a street fight. The Beryllium dissipates. The bacteria slows down and then stops and free floats. Soon a second cell repeats this process. Then another. It's working. Beth's eyes widen. Jack smiles and slaps his hands together. "Fuck yeah!" he shouts.

"This would probably kill a healthy person," Beth soberly concludes.

"You're right. Get more doses ready," Jack responds. Beth returns to the work station and fills more syringes.

At the moment the only thing that matters is trying to save Rachel. Jack realizes for the first time that in spite of his outer delinquent attitude, he loves these people. They are like family to him. Saving Rachel to Jack is tantamount to saving himself. They have always been kind to him.Always welcomed him with open arms. Made him feel safe. Allowed him to be who he is so he could grow. He never appreciated that until this moment. Now he has a chance to do something for them. He has to take it.

Back in medical, Lorna runs her face under the eye wash station. She sobs in pain and looks like death warmed over. She sobs uncontrollably as she realizes there is something really wrong with her. The only thing she can think to do is wash it out. She has to clean it out. She doesn't have time to get to a hospital. What the fuck did that asshole Jason give me? she thinks to herself. She looks at herself in the mirror, and it's not getting any better. She convulses and vomits red and black tar into the sink. She cries out. She looks in the sink and she sees a tooth. She looks up at the mirror in horror at the absence of a tooth on the bottom row.

She reaches slowly for the next tooth. It splits off at her touch. Her eyes bulge and tears fill her reddening eye sockets. She convulses and vomits a large clump of blood and stomach tissue. She shakes violently in fear and holds the sink for support as her legs fall out from under her. She looks up at her face in the mirror and her nose looks crooked. She imagines it's the trauma getting to her. She touches it and it moves. Her eyes bulge again and she takes it in her fingers. It comes off in her hand. She screams as blood floods from her nose into the sink. She gets woozy and her eyes roll back into her head and she collapses, slamming her head on the sink on the way down. Her right eye flies off her face into the corner of the bathroom. She lies motionless with blood and pus running from her eye socket and the hole that once housed her nose.

The red orbs the mouse sees through surveys the animals in the holding area. It approaches another mouse. The live mouse sniffs it. The zombie mouse clamps down on the live mouse's throat and blood splatters the cage around it. Splatter hits a bunny and an ape in the mouth. The live mouse collapses in the zombie mouse's grip. The mouse clamps down hard, severing the live mouse's head as the torso rolls to the side. The zombie mouse buries its head in the torso and slurps loudly.

The bunny writhes and kicks out the door to its cage. Its eyes turn red and it bleeds from the mouth. It hops to a dog cage and attacks the dog. The ape breaks out of its cage and attacks the ape in the cage in front. Blood sprays around the holding area as animal after animal attack one another. The first zombie dog disembowels a live bunny. A zombie ape rips the head off a bunny. They attack each other. The holding area turns into a slaughterhouse. No survivors. Surveillance monitors document the horror.

In the break room, Jason lays motionless. Then a convulsion. He twitches. His red, pus filled eyes open. He rises. He stares at nothing. He lowly growls and surveys the room. He turns toward the exit. An intern walks by and notices Jason. The intern spies Jason's grotesque eyes and quickly scampers away. Jason lumbers to follow.

The Barrister Institute Security Control Center is a large, glass encased enclosure with a fifteen foot security console which monitors all goings on at the facility. It also has three individual work stations with computers and a small arms locker.

Parker sits at a console monitoring the ladies' locker room video feeds. Thanks to the work of the now intelligent zombie mouse, the alarms in animal holding are out of commission, so Parker is unaware there is a problem there. Given the institute's 300+ cameras, if he's not looking for the issue, he won't see it.

Plus the institute has a very small security staff since they've never needed one.

Cliff strolls in and approaches the small arms locker. He opens it and removes a Glock 22 and two clips. This draws Parker's attention. "Sir?" he inquires.

"Logan Gibson from Hicks is in the building. I want to know where he goes and what he does. Radio me if anything odd happens," Cliff instructs.

"Yes sir," Parker says and he rises and heads out of the office. Jack and Beth both enter.

"Tell me you have something Jack," Cliff presses. Jack nods.

"It's a hail Mary but…" Jack replies.

"I'll take whatever you got," Cliff says.

Cliff grabs a second gun and hands it to Jack. This takes Jack by surprise. "What's this for?" inquires Jack, looking shocked.

"There is an issue in animal holding. It's contained for the moment, but we can't let this get out. I'm trying to contain it, but Logan is here from Hicks poking his nose around. So we need to protect ourselves if things get dicey," Cliff instructs. Beth and Jack stare slack jawed at Cliff. Jack nods that he understands.

"If it comes to that, head shots only. Let's hope it doesn't come to that," Jack replies. Cliff taps Jack's shoulder. They stuff the weapons in the back of their pants under their shirts so they aren't detected. They exit.

They rush through the halls. "Give me the quick and dirty," Cliff commands.

"Hypo cocktail of ammonium salt and Prednisone for the Beryllium and Ciprofloxacin for the bacteria. In the dead ape it showed promise," Jack summarizes. Cliff nods.

"Give me the syringe," Cliff demands. Jack's eyes widen in disbelief.

"I should do this," Jack replies, worried that Cliff is too close to the situation.

"I'm going in alone. If we're wrong and something goes bad, you know what to do," Cliff explains. Jack studies Cliff for a moment, trying to work out if his logic is sound. Satisfied that he really has no choice right now, he taps Cliff's back and hands him the syringe. Beth hugs Cliff and tears up. "Whatever happens sweetie, it'll be alright. Stay here with Jack," Cliff comforts Beth.

"I love you daddy. It'll work," she squeaks through a sob.

"If we can reverse the effect, we might be able to restart her body systems. She's only been gone a few hours," Cliff theorizes. Jack's jaw opens.

"This is nuts," Jack exclaims, trying to wrap his brain around this crazy science fiction stuff. Cliff chuckles.

"We're pioneers Jack. Pioneers," Cliff reassures Jack. Jack smiles.

Cliff carefully enters the room and addresses Rachel's angry corpse with caution. He shuts the door slowly and deadbolts it. Beth grabs Jack's hand for comfort. She has so many conflicting emotions the gesture will hopefully keep her sane. Cliff slowly approaches Rachel. His fear of the unknown and the monster before are all overridden by a more powerful force. He's loved Rachel his whole adult life. Risking his own to get her back is a trade he would make every single time. He fearfully takes another step. The fear of dying right now is second to losing her. It's not rational, but it's his reality. Jack squeezes Beth's hand. In his helpless state of observation, Jack feels compelled to help in some way. It manifests in Beth's grasp. Beth is not even aware of it but it makes her feel better.

Rachel lunges against the restraints to get to Cliff. His blood calls to her like a glass of water to someone dying of thirst. Cliff carefully unsheathes the syringe. It's tougher to do with rubber gloves on than it looks. He stops and looks back at Beth and Jack. This is the moment of truth. Cliff can almost see his life pass in front of his eyes. He knows he is just as likely to die at Rachel's hand as save her. But he wouldn't have it any other way. The pain of going on without her is too much to bear. He tearfully smiles at Beth as if to say goodbye. Beth puts her hand on the glass to gesture her love and admiration for her daddy. She has never been more proud, nor more horrified than this very moment. Beth and Jack nod yes to Cliff. They're acknowledging what Cliff needs to do as well as the risk he faces right now. Cliff turns back to Rachel. It's time.

CHAPTER 17

Cliff inches his way toward Rachel. She lunges for his arm. He dodges her. Cliff checks the vitals monitor. Brain activity is off the charts. He glances at the micro camera monitor. The compound swims in her veins like a rushing river in anticipation of a fresh source of nourishment.

He picks up a cup from the table with the blood he was feeding her with and tosses it at her face, smothering her lips and neck area. Rachel loses interest in Cliff for a brief moment as she slurps the sweet hemoglobin nectar from her lips. Cliff quickly injects the needle into her thigh and drains its contents and backs away quickly. This got Rachel's attention and the hostile reception that comes with being stuck with a needle while you weren't looking.

The compound dances in the monitor. It changes direction as if either chasing something or running from something. Rachel twitches as hostility is replaced with involuntary muscle spasms. Cliff shoots a wide eyed expression at Jack. Jack's eyes also widen. Something is definitely happening. This is good news. The vitals monitor spikes brain activity. Cliff studies her carefully. He inches a crash cart next to the bed. He hopes he won't have to fight her.

The micro camera monitor suddenly goes dark. They are flying semi blind. Rachel writhes as if in pain. Cliff, Jack and Beth are trying to figure out if this is helping or hurting. The vital monitor broadcasts quite a battle raging in Rachel's brain. Then just as quickly as it started, it levels out. Rachel slowly calms. Her arms rest at her side and her head rests against the pillow behind her. Her eyes close.

Cliff suddenly panics that they've killed her again. He pants and inches toward the bed. His own heart is beating so fast his head could explode at any minute from the trauma of this whole surreal ordeal. Beth covers her mouth assuming Rachel died. Jack touches the glass. He tears up. Rachel does not move. Cliff approaches the bed. He touches her arm. She does not react. He stares at her for a minute. She lies still. He pulls the chair close to the bed and sits down. He takes her hand in his and weeps softly. Beth buries her head in Jack's chest. Jack warmly holds her and comforts her.

Rachel's eyes twitch and open. Cliff does not notice through his tears. Jack notices and taps the glass gently. Cliff looks back. Jack frantically points at Rachel. Cliff whips around and sees Rachel's open eyes. They are not red orbs. They are her eyes. She looks over at Cliff. Cliff stands suddenly and leans over the bed. "Rachel?" he calls out. Rachel's eyes widen.

"Cliff," she replies with a weak, raspy hum. Jack smiles big and Beth puts both her hands on the glass and cries out in happy sobs.

Cliff puts a drop of water on Rachel's dry, zombie like lips. She accepts it and coughs. Cliff removes the restraints from her arms and embraces her. "Oh my God, Rachel," Cliff cries. He lifts her dead weight and holds her close to him. This is the new happiest and saddest moment of his whole life. He looks at the vitals monitor. It isn't registering any activity other than brain activity. The micro camera reveals hardly any movement. Cliff looks back at Jack. Jack, being as clueless as Cliff when it comes to this scenario, simply smiles and shrugs his shoulders, telling Cliff to just enjoy the moment. Cliff looks into Rachel's eyes.

"Let me go," Rachel whispers. Cliff's smile is immediately replaced by worry.

"What?" he asks as if he can't believe what she said. He draws close to her.

"Let me go," she admonishes with more force this time. Cliff can't believe it.

"Jack and Beth brought you back. We've killed it," negotiates Cliff. Rachel looks lovingly at him. A bloody tear forms around her eye.

"You have to kill me," she pleads. Cliff tears up.

"What? You can't ask me to do that," Cliff insists.

"I'm aware," Rachel advises. Cliff looks at her like she's not making any sense.

"Aware of what baby?" Cliff inquires dreadfully.

"My body is dead. But I'm not. I feel everything it feels. I feel its need for blood. I crave to feed like it does," she explains. Cliff's eyes bulge in horror. He looks back at Jack and Beth as if asking what to do. Jack stares blankly back, knowing he has no idea how to help her.

"We're going to kill it," he assures Rachel.

"We don't have much time. It's fighting back. I can feel it. I can't stop it. You're the only one who can end my suffering," Rachel begs. Cliff can't say anything. The tears roll down his cheek.

"I can't. I can't...let you go," Cliff sobs. Rachel twitches. She looks lovingly at her husband who she has loved as long as she can remember.

"I love you darling. You'll get through this. You'll find the answers. You must save Beth. You must take care of her. We will always be together my love," Rachel lovingly expresses. Brain activity spikes in the vitals monitor. Beth sobs uncontrollably. Jack holds her.

"Baby, no," Cliff begs. She smiles at him.

"Save me my love," she quietly pleads.

Suddenly her body violently twitches. The micro camera springs to life with new circulation. The coloring is different but the compound's signature is undeniable. Cliff stands. Rachel's eyes gloss over. "Rachel? Baby?! No. Please!!" Cliff shouts. Beth screams. Jack holds her close. Cliff sobs. Rachel's red orbs return and scope the room. She spies Cliff next to her. She lunges for him. He leaps back. "Rachel, fight it! You gotta fight baby!!" Cliff yells. Rachel reaches down with her freed arms and rips the straps off her legs. She twists herself to a seated position and thrusts her legs off the bed.

Jack bangs the glass. "She's gone Cliff! Get the hell out of there!" screams Jack. Cliff back peddles slowly. Rachel stands and locks in on Cliff. Jack slams the glass and tries to bash in the door unsuccessfully against the dead bolt. Cliff backs to the door. Rachel pursues a step at a time. Measuring him up like a steak she can't quite decide which angle to start with. "You have to shoot her Cliff!" Jack screams. Cliff shakes his head no. "Do it!!" Jack continues.

"Daddy!" Beth cries out. Cliff turns and observes Beth's helpless and hopeless gaze.

Cliff removes the gun from his pants and lifts it toward Rachel. She growls softly and takes another step. Cliff holds the gun out from him. Rachel reaches for his hand. He dodges the effort. "Do it now Cliff!" Jack commands. Cliff's shaky hands aim for her forehead. He sobs. She's only a few feet away.

"Daddy, please," Beth begs, sobbing. Cliff shrieks in emotional agony as Rachel reaches back to swing at his hand again. He fires the gun which punctures her head just above her nose and explodes out the back of her head just as she was reaching around to swipe him. Her skull and brains spray the room behind her with a black pus filled goo along with bone fragments and bits of blackened brain matter.

Rachel drops backwards as if a stiff wind took her and her body plops the floor. Beth screams. Cliff drops to his knees.

It wasn't bad enough that Cliff lost his love. It's worse that he thought he lost her, then had her back for a moment, and then lost her again. He sits against the door in shock and stunned silence. He replays the moment in his mind again and again, trying to see some different choice that could have saved her. Something else that would have changed the outcome. There is nothing. This fucking organism has come into their lives and was destroying everything he ever cared for. He has always been in control. But this time, he has never been more out of control. He doesn't know what to do anymore. All he has left now is Beth and Jack. He realizes now how much he actually cares for Jack. He loves him like his own son. It's funny how random tragedy wakes you up to the truth of who you are. But there it is. He's always seen through Jack's walls and knew who he was. Because he used to be Jack. He used to be just like Jack. And it was Rachel who helped him grow up and mature. Now Jack has Beth. And in that moment, Cliff knows what his purpose is now. Whether he lives or dies is no longer important. But if he can save his little girl and the young man she loves so much, that is a purpose worth going on for.

Cliff reaches behind and unlocks the door. Jack opens it and checks Rachel. She's not moving. The vital stats monitor reveals no brain activity and the micro camera reveals pooling of the organism. They haven't found a way to kill it yet. But they're on the right track. Beth falls into Cliff's arms and they sob and hold one another. Jack sits with them and Cliff holds Jack's shoulder. They comfort each other through the tragic loss of the most important person in their world.

CHAPTER 18

In Cliff's office, Logan types at Cliff's computer. He knows where Cliff keeps his password and gains access to the project files.He carefully studies the data on the ZnMBe project. His mouth opens wide and his eyes light up like it's Christmas morning. He smiles and reaches into his pocket and retrieves a flash drive.

The lab door to his right opens slowly and Jason slowly plods through it, red orb eyes fixated on Logan. Logan is so preoccupied with the flash drive to notice. Logan installs the flash drive into the computer and commands it to download the files onto the drive. The computer hums in compliance. Jason inches closer to Logan. His undead gait is consistent in its methodical constant.The files load quickly on to the flash drive.

Jason trips over a lamp power cord, causing it to tumble to the ground. This grabs Logan's attention.He springs up and dodges a violent swing from Jason. Jason lunges for Logan and they wrestle over the desk, knocking the contents to the floor. Jason one arms Logan into the air at the back window. Logan bounces off it and slams the ground hard. He struggles to lose the cobwebs. Before he can rise, Jason pounces on him. Logan punches at Jason but it doesn't faze him. Jason is much stronger than Logan. Logan uses all of his strength to get Jason off him but Jason's head falls at Logan's side. It's all the access Jason needs as he locks his teeth on Logan's side. Logan screams in pain and elbows Jason in the head to get him to let go. Logan tries to stand but Jason grabs his ankle and crunches his lower leg with his teeth. Logan screams again and falls next to Jason. Logan swings at Jason again but Jason is ready this time and catches his arm and removes a large chunk of his forearm.

Logan suddenly starts convulsing. He wants to get up but has no motor control and can feel himself choking on his own blood.

In Med Lab, Lorna twitches. Her red orbs open and she sits up. She stands and looks around the room. She exits Med Lab. A male tech walks by and looks up just in time to find Lorna throw herself at him. For a split second the tech thinks it's his lucky day, but staring into her dead red orbs with her missing nose and eye he quickly realizes he's in deep shit. Lorna opens her mouth and approaches his face. He grotesquely turns away only to leave his neck exposed. As if that was the reaction she was seeking, Lorna opens his neck up like a vampire with no etiquette. Blood sprays Lorna's face and the wall behind them. The tech screams and writhes but Lorna pins him to the ground and bites off his cheek, exposing his left upper and lower teeth. Blood pours from the wound as the tech slowly slumps and then convulses.

A second tech pulls Lorna off the first tech, who writhes on the floor. Lorna turns to the second tech and attacks his face. She pulls away with his left eye crunching in her teeth. The tech screams and throws Lorna to the ground. She looks back at him and he punches her. Then he starts convulsing. Black pus and slimy mucus rush from his eye socket down over his mouth. He breathes some of it in and flails his body against the back wall. He violently throws up blood and tissue as he collapses, convulsing.

In the animal housing area, the animals break out of their cages. Two female techs walk by the outside of the room where the carnage is happening, and drop their files at the jail break. The animals scurry around the holding area, bouncing off walls.

They rip the first aid kit off the wall. Another destroys the necropsy cart.

In Observation Room B, Cliff, Jack and Beth console one another at Rachel's passing. Beth sobs softly into Cliff's chest. Jack touches Cliff's shoulder. "I'm so sorry," Jack consoles through teary eyes. Cliff tears up in response. Cliff rises up and picks Beth up. Jack stands with him.

"I need to go to my office," Cliff advises softly. Jack nods yes in response. They exit the room and Cliff closes the door and locks it.

Back in animal holding, the female techs outside the room watch the animals freak out inside. Tech one spies the alarm button, unfortunately located inside the holding room by the sink. Tech 2 looks at her with wide eyes and shakes her head no. The last thing either of them need is to get attacked by these animals. But something has to be done. Tech one types the code to unlock the door and rushes in, making a beeline for the sink. Little did she know a red orbed ape was tracking her every move and tackles her the second she stepped in the room.

Tech two screams but sees a seam and makes a run for the sink. She gets there and launches at the alarm button. A pus eyed dog takes notice and pounces. The alarm blares loudly and the door closes. But before it has a chance to seal, the dog that attacked the second tech knocks a crash cart over heading for her and it lands in the doorway, preventing the holding area from being sealed.

Cliff, Beth and Jack stop dead in their tracks at the sound of the alarm blaring. "That's the alarm from animal holding," Cliff surmises. He races to the house phone on the near wall and grabs the receiver and presses zero. "It's me. What's going on?" Cliff demands. Cliff looks at Jack wide eyed. He hangs up slowly. "There is a break out in animal holding. They're all showing signs of rabies. Red glazed eyes and they're loose," Cliff summarizes nervously.

"How?" Jack inquires, not realizing the zombie mouse was out and about.

"I don't know. But the animal holding alarm automatically locks the facility down so nothing can get in or out. The only way to override it is at the Control Center," Cliff advises. Jack stops for a moment and thinks.

"Somehow the compound got loose. Maybe it's airborne. Maybe something else got infected," Jack says, trying to work out the logic.

"The mouse," Beth interjects. "Has anyone seen the mouse since the ape attacked mom?" she continues. Jack's eyes widen.

"Fuck me. We could already be totally screwed." Jack exclaims.

"Let's get to Control and find out how bad it is," Cliff commands. They head for Control.

Motorized blast doors descend over all the exterior doors and chains over the windows to the facility. The parking garage cages cover the exits. Elevators shut down. The facility goes into lock down.

In animal holding, the female tech who sprang the alarm surveys the room. Infected animals run wild around the room chaotically. She searches for the other tech. She's writhing on the floor in the corner. She turns to the exit. The crash cart is stuck in the door jam. But it's a way out. She bolts for the door. She puts her leg over the cart but an infected ape grabs her hair. She screams and struggles. The ape tosses her across the room by her hair, yanking a large chunk out by the root. The tech screams furiously. A dog clamps down on her throat and squeezes. She gurgle breathes and wrestles the dog. The dog finally loosens its grip and she kicks it off. She feels a sting between her legs. She lifts her lab coat and two mice are burrowing themselves into her underwear. She screams and hits one, knocking it back. The other mouse weasels through her underwear into her vaginal canal. She screams and writhes to get it out but it's already too late. Red and black liquid gush from her vaginal canal through her underwear. She convulses and her eyes roll back into her head. Her abdomen bobs and shakes as the mouse continues to feed through her abdominal cavity. She collapses and twitches.

The ape spies the opening in the door where the crash cart is stuck. It slowly approaches it. A dog leaps over it and through the hole. The animals all file out as if they were on fire. Staff members in the hallway take off running. None of them are fast enough to escape the animals.Anape tackles a cook. He bites off his ear. The cook screams. The ape reaches into the cook's mouth and forces his hand down his throat. The cook struggles and his eyes bulge as he gurgle screams. The ape growls loudly and yanks the cook's throat out of his mouth. The cook immediately goes limp and blood and tissue ooze from his mouth and nostrils as his dead eyes stare at nothing.

A dog chases down a nurse and clips her Achilles heel. She screams and hits the deck. The dog opens its jaw wide and clamps down on her temples. She reaches for her head and tries to get the dog off. The dog tightens its grip. The nurse convulses and her eyes roll back into her head. The dog clamps again and her face contorts as her skull caves in. Her eye pops out followed by blood and brain matter. The dog howls.

The animals race in every direction taking down dozens of staff members. The first staff members to die suddenly rise, infected by the compound and head off to find new donors. The animals continue their search and widen their strike area.

The compound has been lying dormant, waiting for the chance at life again. Now it has it and it's growing. If it wasn't for the ice age maybe it would have decimated the earth. Like all living things, the bacteria just wants to live. In that, man is its enemy. But it has no empathy. It has no remorse. It can't be negotiated with. It's coming. It wants to survive and it doesn't care about the consequences of its actions. Ironically, when it comes to man, they often share that trait. In that a human being could almost empathize. At least they would if it weren't for the fact the bacteria was trying to kill them all.

CHAPTER 19

Cliff, Beth and Jack race through a hallway on their way to Control. Staff members run by them heading the opposite direction screaming. "How did the mouse infect the animals? How is that even possible?" Beth frantically asks. Jack looks at her like she's not going to like his answer.

"When the ape attacked your mom. The only way out of that room was the door, or the ventilation system. If you know your way around, you can get anywhere in the facility. It recalled where it came from. So many animals, so much blood in one place. Didn't take much," Jack somberly admits. Cliff shoots a look at Jack. Jack is insinuating the fucking compound is intelligent. That it remembers. That it knows. How is that possible? Cliff can only ponder this horror. If they have any hope of figuring out how to kill it, they have to get out of the institute alive first.

As Cliff realizes the scope of the situation, he stops. Jack and Beth halt with him. "What?" Jack asks.

"We have to notify the CDC," replies Cliff. Jack's eyes widen huge.

"You haven't told the CDC?" Jack grumbles.

"It's complicated. Not everything is simple when a government agency is involved," explains Cliff. Beth covers her mouth in shame. She can't believe her father would do anything outside of the law. She's horrified.

"Daddy, what did you do?" she asks teary eyed.

Cliff frowns at Beth. He looks away in shame. Lying to the CDC. A sin by omission if not a sin by commission. But Cliff also knows there are other powers in play. Powers that even influence the CDC. And Cliff knows if they do this prematurely, greater consequences are possible. But Cliff knows he can't say a word about this to either of them. Beth feels the nausea of shame gut punch her. Jack pulls his cell phone out. "What are you doing?" Cliff inquires.

"Calling 9-1-1." Jack replies frantically.

"Cell phones don't work at Barrister. Disrupts research equipment. We have to get to a landline,"Cliff explains. This just gets better and better Jack thinks. Cliff has fucked this up royally and as brilliant as Jack is, he's not sure he can get them out of this. He glares at Cliff. "Let's just fix this," Cliff pleads.

Logan turns the corner ahead, moving slowly. His eyes are glossed over red orbs. Jack's eyes widen. "Fuck me," he stutters in disbelief.

"Oh my God," exclaims Beth. Cliff looks pale for a moment. Two things about this sight become clear to Cliff in an instant. He has way bigger problems than dealing with Hicks now. And the second is he has to put Logan down.

"He's turned, Cliff," advises Jack. Cliff looks at Jack. Logan spots Cliff and slowly makes a beeline for him. Cliff lifts his gun at Logan.

"I never wanted it to be this way Logan. God damn it," Cliff says struggling to pull the trigger.

"Cliff?" Jack inquires hesitantly. Cliff sighs heavily just as Logan leans out to touch him. Cliff fires. The round annihilates Logan's right eye, blowing out the back of his skull. Brain matter and black bloody pus cover the floor and back wall behind Logan, who crumbles to a knee and lumbers to the floor like a sack of potatoes.

"This is getting out of control," Jack exclaims like Captain Obvious. Jack pulls his gun from his waist and the three of them continue on toward Control. Institute personnel race past them in a panic. Infected staff pursue slowly. Cliff and Jack raise their guns and drop them one by one. The deafening sound of gun fire, spent shells clanging on the floor, the squish of people and infected traipsing through blood, brain, pus and fecal waste. Killing people isn't like what you see in the movies. And the movies don't get it right when zombies die. There is a loss of dignity even in their death. The irony of the phrase zombies dying seems comically ironic to Jack in a tragic way. They've seen a thousand zombie movies and told a thousand gross zombie jokes. They've referred to ugly coeds as zombies and made fun of people on social media. The cliché is as old as the zombie lore, but none of that compares to the real life indignity of shitting your pants even though your body is dead. It's like ZnMBe has a thing or two in common with mere mortals. The sight is sickening.

Cliff turns the corner of the next hallway and peeks through the maze of bodies to his office door down the hall. He stops Jack and Beth. "We need to get the files on the compound from my office," he instructs Jack.

"I got it," Jack replies. Jack hugs the wall and makes it to the door. He takes a step to enter and an infected assistant greets him with hunger in her infected eyes. Jack is caught by surprise and ducks to the left, rolls on his back and leaps up from the far side of this middle aged undead creature. She turns her head to him and Jack shoots a round into her forehead. She drops like a stone.

Jack races into the office around the desk and sits at Cliff's computer. Cliff and Beth reach the door and enter. Cliff silently closes the door behind him. Jack notices a flash drive already sticking out of the computer with the Hicks logo on it. Jack looks at Cliff. Cliff walks around the desk and checks it. "See what's on it," Cliff whispers. Jack opens the drive directory. The ZnMBe files fill the computer screen.

"Holy shit," Jack quietly exclaims. Cliff realizes Logan was in the process of stealing the files on the compound. He was going to take it to Hicks and leave Cliff completely out of it, or worse. The revelation produces a sickening feeling in Cliff's stomach. He never trusted Logan or Hicks, but he never expected them to betray him on that level. In that sense Cliff feels a sudden relief that Logan is now dead, and at his hand no less. And that feeling of relief makes Cliff feel a little sick at his lack of humanity. For all of his faults, Cliff wouldn't betray someone that way or wish them dead. He has always had his humanity. But at the moment the line is blurry for him. Right now, though, they need to get out of this alive first. He can contemplate his humanity all he wants once they're all safe again. In the meantime, there is a facility full of people he used to know who are now suffering immeasurably at his hand. That is something he has to live with. And that is the bigger problem. All he can do is end their suffering. He owes them that much. But that means doing the unthinkable. The dynamics of the situation are impossible to process for anyone. So Cliff puts those thoughts to bed for the moment. He needs to save Beth now. If he can do that, perhaps there is hope for his humanity after all.

Jack opens an analysis file and a graphic fills the screen with data and spiking curve. "Oh God," Jack exclaims. Cliff looks at the computer. "The incubation period is exponentially shortening. It's adapted to our body chemistry and now the reaction time is down to seconds, not hours like with Rachel," Jack explains. Cliff pounds his fist on the desk.

"We have to call the CDC," Cliff says.

He lifts the receiver. There is no dial tone. "We still have internet. I can email Doctor Norris," Jack offers. Cliff looks at Jack for a long moment. He nods approval.

"And take the flash drive," Cliff instructs. Jack opens a new email from Cliff and composes.

"Dr. Norris, toxic bacterial compound security breach at Barrister. In lock down. No phone service. We have the research files and are close to a solution. But we ran out of time as outbreak at the institute has infected most staff already and spreading fast. Containment protocol recommended. Infection spread through bite or fluids. Incubation period accelerated to just seconds now. No time to find a solution. Need assistance ASAP."

Jack sends the email and grabs the flash drive and shoves it in his pocket. He looks at Cliff for direction. "How did it come to this? I can't believe any of this. All these people," Cliff somberly confesses. Beth wraps her arms around Cliff. She weeps softly on his shoulder. A tear runs down Cliff's cheek. He never wanted any of this. He wanted to help people. Jack touches his shoulder.

"The best thing we can do for these people is to end their suffering and do all we can to make sure this doesn't happen again. We have to warn people and work to find a solution to kill it. We need to get out of here alive," Jack counsels Cliff. His words shock himself as much as they shock Cliff. Whether it's the circumstances of the day or his responsibility for bringing the material to the facility in the first place, his maturation curve has to accelerate just to have a chance at survival. Jack didn't even know how strong he was. The question is whether it's enough.

CHAPTER 20

The Power Control Room is located on the basement level of the institute. It's a rather large sub facility, covering 300 feet on all sides. As you would imagine, it's not aesthetically pleasing at all with off white barren walls enclosing a series of air handlers, breaker boxes and transformer units, a secured 30 foot by 25 foot control room featuring a large control panel with live video relays. Two techs man the room 24 hours a day to ensure everything runs smoothly at the institute from an infrastructure perspective. On the current shift those two unlucky men are Joe and Dave. Joe is the supervisor and Dave is the tech. Each day Dave is tasked with performing rounds to check for issues, system instability, security breaches and any suspicious activity. He carries a police baton and flashlight with him.

When the alarms went off in animal control, Joe sent Dave out to the outer entrance of Power Control to keep security over the area. Dave walks the perimeter of the area checking for issues. A red orb eyed mouse spies him from the vent shaft above. The mouse stalks its next source of nourishment like a lion stalking a gazelle.

Dave walks by the entrance door to the control area and a loud thump shakes the door. Dave stands motionless. Another thump rocks his world. "Please let us in!" screams a voice on the outside of the door. Dave stands motionless, breathing hard. Piercing screams and sounds of gurgled guttural noises follow. A small flow of blood trickles its way under the door jam. That is followed by an eerie, uncomfortable silence. Dave shines his light on the blood under the door and his breathing pace increases. He clicks on the walkie talkie hanging from his shirt collar. "What the fuck is going on out there, Joe? I think I got blood here." Dave whispers in a panic.

"Don't worry about it, just don't open the door," breathes Joe.

Dave shines his flash light around the room. He senses something coming for him but attributes it to his mind playing tricks on him like watching a horror movie. He talks to himself to convince himself he's secure here. A creaking noise interrupts his thought process from the next corridor. He slows his breathing so he can listen closely. A scraping noise. He bolts his light in that direction. He sees nothing. He creeps toward the sound ever so slowly, ready to turn back and run at the first sign of trouble. He turns the corner and proceeds along a hallway with pipes on both walls from floor to ceiling, some periodically releasing steam pressure.

He pauses for a moment to listen. There is no noise. Then he hears a clicking noise like the sound of hoof beats. He stops. He shines his flashlight down the corridor. A set of bright red eyes attached to a zombified dog turn from around the next corner. The dog growls lowly. Dave slowly steps back. A clicking noise from behind him. A chill runs down his spine. He wipes sweat from his brow as he turns behind him slowly and deliberately as if to avoid making any noise to stay undetected from monsters lurking in the shadows. Another dog stares at him through its glowing orbs. He stands frozen, pondering what move he can make to save himself. Something clinks the pipe to his right. His eyes bulge as he slowly turns just his eyes to the right. Anape with red orbs hangs upside down from the ceiling. It squeals and drops down on his shoulder. The dogs attack from both sides.

Dave hits the deck. He wrestles with the animals attacking him, taking large chunks of meat from his arms, legs and abdomen. The mouse launches itself from the pipes above and lands in Dave's screaming mouth. It burrows its way down his throat. Dave stops moving as his eyes gloss over red. Blood and tissue spatter from his mouth and nose. The mouse burrows a hole in his throat and crawls out, dripping in red pus and bodily fluid.

Joe scopes out the monitors in the control room. He's lost sight of Dave. "Dave, come in." Joe speaks into the microphone. He gets no response. A flash blurs by one monitor. Joe reacts too late to see what it was. Then another monitor shows an ape fly by on the pipes. Joe's eyes light up. "Dave, come the fuck in. Where are you?" Joe says in a half panic. Dave plods by a monitor slowly heading back to the control room. Joe sees him and tries to figure out why the fuck he's moving like that. "Are you OK? What's wrong?" Joe calls again. He again gets no response.

Joe loses Dave on the monitors again and then a loud bang on the door to the control room interrupts his concentration. Joe looks at the door. "Dave?" Joe cries out. Bang! Joe jumps a bit. He slowly creeps to the door. Bang! Bang! The door noise is creepy as fuck and Joe reaches it and looks through the security hole. He sees the top of Dave's hat. "Fuck me dude, why you gotta pull that shit?" Joe screams at Dave as he opens the door and heads back to the console. He assumes Dave was playing a prank. Dave looks up as Joe walks away and he launches himself at Joe, tackling him to the floor. Joe struggles and screams. Dave bites Joe's arm. Joe screams. Dave reaches under Joe's ribcage and in one swinging motion rips Joe's diaphragm straight through. Joe immediately screams and then stops as his lungs no longer fill with air. Dave wraps his teeth around Joe's stomach and removes a giant bloody patch of intestines. Blood gurgles up through his mouth as his eyes deaden and then turn red and gloss over.

Dave rises and peruses the room. He walks over to the electric control room. He opens the door and enters. A rat races behind a control box with several wires coming out of it. Dave follows. Dave's foot gets stuck in the cords and he fights to free it. His shirt gets stuck on the panel lock and he rips open the panel, freeing his shirt. The rat is on a pipe behind the panel. Dave puts his hand through the panel to reach the rat. The electric shock launches Dave backward into a breaker panel. The panel explodes and lights Dave on fire. His blood, brain and tissue spray in every direction as his body flails to get free and then stops.

In Cliff's office, Cliff unlocks the locker behind his desk. He reaches for a taser and a PR24 baton. Jack raises his eyebrows to Cliff. Cliff shrugs at the gesture that those are meaningless weapons against these undead things. As zombie apocalypse weapons go, Cliff is clearly an amateur. But Cliff likes to think of himself as an improviser.The lights go out. "Seriously?" Beth exclaims sarcastically. She can't help but to think they are living every zombie movie she's ever watched. Cliff stumbles over a trash can on his way to the cabinet near the door. He opens it. A flashlight illuminates the front half of the room. Cliff shines it in the cabinet and grabs a second one and hands it to Beth.

"We need to get the power back on," Cliff advises.

"Why?" Jack asks. It's not that Jack likes the power off, but the way Cliff said it makes it sound pretty bad that it's off.

"We can't set the self destruct without it," Cliff reveals.

"Self destruct?" Beth whispers harshly. Cliff looks warmly at Beth.

"These people are already dead on the outside. We can't save them. But we can stop their suffering and prevent this from spreading," Cliff summarizes. Beth tears up and looks away. The biting truth is Cliff's right and she knows it. She hates that he's right, but he is. Jack takes Beth's face in his hands gently and kisses her softly.

"We're going to get through this," he tells her reassuringly. Beth wipes her tears and smiles weakly at Jack.

"Let's go," Cliff commands.

Cliff opens the office door slowly. There is no movement in the hallway. The walls are covered in blood and another substance they can't identify which looks like black chunky paint. Jack leads the way with his flashlight. Emergency lights barely illuminate the hallway but even those have blood caked on the light guards, which adds a rosy hue to the dim light. It's just enough to up the creep factor. They turn the corner ahead. It's quiet enough to hear their hearts beating. That, in and of itself, freaks them out. They involuntarily try to quiet their breathing so as not to draw attention to themselves.

Jack hears movement around the next corner. He raises his fist and they all stop. He shines his light at the corridor. Nothing. He shines it to the other side and nothing. He shines back to the original side and Jason is standing right in front of Jack. His red orb eyes study Jack like a sandwich to a starving man. He licks his lips and grabs Jack and throws him up against the wall. Jack shrieks and cries out in pain as he thumps to the floor. Jack's flashlight clanks to the floor. The light shines the top of Jack's head. Beth screams. Jack shakes off the cobwebs as Jason pounces on top of him. In his semi-dazed state, Jack half fantasized Jason would do this without being infected over his jealousy of Beth's affections. But this is worse. Jason snaps his jaws at Jack's head and arms. Jack fights him off. Jack tries to grip his gun but Jason swats it away as they wrestle.

Beth backs into the wall behind her and runs into the fire hose chamber handle. She quickly turns to look to see what it was and her flashlight finds the hose with an axe mounted over it. She uses the butt of her flashlight to smash the glass and grabs the axe. Cliff tries to pull Jason off Jack but Jason throws him off with a shrug of the shoulder. Cliff falls backwards into the hallway. Jason punches Jack, dazing him. Jack raises his arm in defense, leaving it vulnerable. Jason opens his jaw wide. Beth swings with all her might and lands the blade side of the axe directly in the top of Jason's head, splitting the top of his head into two dangling sections. Jason's arms fall limp. Jack quickly slithers out from under Jason as blackened blood, tissue and pus drip from the six inch gash in his head to the floor. Jason's body clumps to the floor like a sack of potatoes. Beth turns to Cliff and he comforts her. She's never killed anyone before, and even in this situation it's the most horrible thing imaginable to Beth. "Thank you," Jack says gratefully. Beth looks up from Cliff's shoulder. She wipes her tears. She shakes her head at Jack. Cliff cleans the flesh and blood from the axe.

The noise drew attention, though. There is movement coming from around the corner. A group of 3 zombies turn the corner and confront the group. Jack lifts his gun and dispatches the first one between the eyes. Cliff swings the axe like a bat and decapitates the next zombie. The third one is Lorna, lost behind her red orbed eyes. She reaches for Beth. They struggle. Beth punches Lorna. Lorna's jaw dislocates. She clacks her now off center jaws together and charges at Beth. Jack yanks Lorna off Beth and tosses her up against the wall and fires a shot into her left eye, exploding the back of her head against the wall. Beth rises slowly. "Thanks," she weakly says. Jack nods and smiles softly to attempt to lighten the life threatening environment they find themselves in. They can't help but to feel sympathy for Lorna, Jason and the rest of these poor people who died when their deaths should have been prevented. But they can debate the humanity once this is all over. Right now, none of them are safe.

CHAPTER 21

Jack, Cliff and Beth snake their way through hallways, avoiding as many undead staffers as possible. Beth discovers how amazingly challenging it is to keep your breathing silent when you're bombarded by both fear and fatigue. They creep up to the corridor where Power Control's entrance is located. The door is clear of zombies. They sneak along, close to the floor, under the window ledges and reach the door. Cliff pulls on the door handle but it doesn't open. "It's locked," Cliff advises.

"Where's the key?" asks Beth.

"The engineer has the only key," Cliff replies in frustration. Jack spies a pad code next to the door with a red light illuminated.

"Does the keypad work even if the power's out?" inquires Jack. Cliff looks at the lock.

"Yes, it has its own separate emergency backup power system. But I don't know the combination," Cliff advises.

Jack holsters his gun in his pants and retrieves the electronic lock pick from his back pocket. "Makes me glad I brought this with me," Jack whispers. He gently pops the faceplate off the lock and connects the leads. He flips the switch and the machine hums and the numbers rotate and lock one at a time until all 5 are locked. The lock turns from red to green. The door lock clicks. Jack smiles. Cliff opens the door. They enter and shut the door quietly behind them.

Cliff shines his flashlight at the main power panel. "Main power is out. The backup generator has to be switched on manually," summarizes Cliff. Cliff searches the back wall for a small panel. He installs a key into a lock on the panel and a switch box pops open. Cliff flips the switch. The panel illuminates and the generator hums to life.He searches for the breaker boxes on the wall and flips them all to the "ON" position.Light fills the room.

The power engineer stands behind Cliff staring at him through red orbs. "Cliff!" Jack yells. The engineer reaches out and grabs Cliff. Cliff drops to the deck and flips himself around. The engineer stalks him. Jack pulls his gun. "No Jack! Not in here!" Cliff screams. Jack looks around the room, taking in the panels and power controls and suddenly realizes if they start shooting in there they could cut the power, and the ability to launch self destruct, with it. Jack takes a running leap and drop kicks the engineer to the deck. Jack lands right next to him. The engineer grabs for Jack's leg. Jack kicks him away. The engineer gets Jack's foot and slams it in his jaw and bites. Jack screams. Cliff picks the axe up and swings it violently at the engineer, shearing his right arm off. It falls to the floor and the engineer loses his grip on Jack. Jack squirms away. Beth picks up a long flat head screwdriver and charges the engineer, who is now in a seated position. She drives the screwdriver through his left ear and her inertia drives it straight out the right side. Black brain matter, blood and pus drip from the business end of the screwdriver as the engineer drops over silently. Beth backs away quickly.

Cliff tends to Jack. Jack removes his shoe. "He didn't break the skin," Jack says in relief.

"Thank God," Cliff sighs. "Holy shit that was close," Cliff continues.

A loud bang of a door swinging open interrupts the moment and Cliff jumps back.Still holding the axe, he holds it up in ready position.Sprinting steps grow closer and closer followed by growling noises. Cliff, Beth and Jack listen closely. Jack rushes to put his shoe back on. A scream as a blur in human form turns the corner. Cliff swings and plants the head of the axe square into Parker's chest. Cliff's eyes bulge as he realizes Parker was running away from the zombies, not as one of them. Parker chokes up blood and drops to his knees. "Oh, Jesus!" Cliff exclaims. Beth screams. Jack leaps up and helps Parker to the floor gently. Tears run down Parker's cheek as he gurgles breath.

"Have to get to self destruct," Parker instructs. Cliff tears up and shakes his head yes as he holds Parker in his arms.

"I'm sorry. I'm so sorry," Cliff squeaks. Parker slowly closes his eyes and goes limp.

Jack rises and embraces Beth. Cliff sits stoically and stares off. "Cliff," Jack calls. Cliff doesn't respond. Jack touches Cliff's shoulder. Cliff looks up weakly. "We have to go," Jack announces softly. Beth looks at Jack and points to Parker. Jack nods at the subliminal notification they have to shoot Parker in the head to prevent him from coming back since he was killed with the zombie blood filled axe. Jack pulls his gun and puts it to Parker's temple. Cliff looks away in stoic shame.

Jack fires.

"Where to Cliff?" Jack asks matter of factly about the location of the Control Room.

"Two wings over. Maybe a hundred yards," Cliff responds. Jack checks his clip. One round left. Cliff approaches a lock box on the far wall and smashes it open with his flashlight, breaking it. He removes a wrench. He hands the axe to Jack. "I'm done with this," he somberly declares. Jack takes the axe and Cliff hands Beth a wrench from the lock box. Beth hugs Cliff. "Let's do this," Cliff says as he picks up a sledgehammer from the locker.

CHAPTER 22

Several black and white vehicles rapidly approach the street corner at the bottom of the hill near the entrance to the institute. Dr. Norris, a tall dark man in his fifties, steps out of the lead van in a HAZMAT suit. He stares at the institute in the distance and studies the grounds using a pair of binoculars. A tech approaches him. "Set up a perimeter. Get local law enforcement to help you," Dr. Norris directs. The tech scurries off looking like an astronaut wrestling with his moon suit.

Cliff, Beth and Jack slowly and carefully exit the Power Control room. They turn the corner and are greeted by three zombies who charge them like starving animals. Jack swings the axe and beheads a formally twenty two year old intern turned infected cannibal. Beth is greeted by a former janitor who pushes her against the wall. She swings the wrench, creating an indentation in the zombie's head. He bleeds from the eyes and nose but charges again. She swings again, nailing him in the eye. One of the wrench edges gets lodged in the eye socket and Beth has to yank it out, creating a crunchy slushy sound as his eye falls out and the zombie collapses. Cliff lifts the sledge to ward off the attack from his zombie. Cliff pushes him back and wildly swings the sledge, driving a hole into the zombie's chest. Blood, muscle and organs cascade from the open wound. Cliff tries to retrieve the hammer, which is embedded in the zombie as it attacks him again. The axe rains down on the zombie's head from behind and splits it in two, showering Cliff with blood and brains. Thankfully Cliff had closed his mouth, but it didn't make this moment any less disgusting and Cliff leans over and upchucks. "Thanks," he praises Jack, half in gratitude and half in sarcasm. Jack tears off a piece of the zombie's shirt and hands it to Cliff.Cliff shoots Jack a WTF look and Jack casually observes, "You got some…stuff, here." Jack points to his cheek and forehead to give Cliff reference. Cliff looks crossly at Jack and looks around. Realizing there is no other way to clean his face at the moment, he carefully uses the torn shirt to wipe the zombie off his face.

The trio inches their way down the hall. In the distance they hear rustling. Jack stops. He peeks around the corner. The Control Room entrance is at the end of the corridor. But a dozen zombies linger between them and the door. There is no way to pass them without confrontation. "Son of a bitch," Cliff whispers.

"There's too many," Jack surmises.

Cliff stares at the wall in thought for a moment as Jack scopes possible alternate routes. "Maybe if we back track there could be another way in there," Jack offers. Cliff shakes his head no.

"That's the only way in. And when the power went out it reset all the electronic locks so you have to have the master code, which the engineer has. And he's dead," Cliff summarizes. Jack looks at the zombie horde and back at Cliff.

"I can hack it, but I need thirty seconds uninterrupted," Jack concludes.

"Yeah," Cliff agrees and nods. He looks at the zombie horde and then down the opposite hallway. He continues, "Alright. I'll take off down this way, lead those bastards past you here and give you a diversion. They'll follow me and clear the corridor for you.That should give you all the time you need." Beth's eyes widen.

"No," she exclaims quietly. Cliff turns to her.

"Sweetheart, we can't make it in there otherwise. We have to end this. You and Jack can do this," Cliff pleads.

"I'm going with you," Beth begs teary eyed. Cliff embraces her warmly. He looks her in the eyes and smiles like the sun had risen on her face.

"We will be together again very soon. But it's too risky right now. I can't lose you too," Cliff says lovingly. Tears roll down both of their cheeks. Cliff hugs Beth tightly and kisses her cheek. Cliff looks at Jack. "At the back of the control room is a service entrance that leads to the basement level and parking garage. Black SUV. You can find it with the key. Get her out. You should have plenty of time. If I'm not there in time, don't wait for me. You know what to do," Cliff instructs and hands Jack his keys. Jack accepts the keys and nods.

Cliff smiles at Beth and takes off down the opposite hall banging on the walls and screaming. This draws the attention of the zombie horde who turn in pursuit. Jack and Beth huddle down near the corner as the horde passes by.

Jack peeks around the corner. The path to the Control Room door is now clear. They creep down the hallway to the lock. Jack retrieves his hack tool and connects the leads. The tool hacks the lock and it turns green and the latch releases. Jack puts the tool in his pocket as a zombie turns the corner. Jack jumps back in surprise. Beth leaps up and swings her wrench with authority, adding a new three inch hole to the zombie's head next to its ear. She grabs the zombie by the back of the head and drives it into the wall. The zombie drops leaving a trail of disgust on the wall.

Jack chuckles through wide eyes. Beth offers her hand to help him up. "You in?" she asks. Jack smiles and nods affirmative. Beth opens the door. They enter the room. Three zombies greet them violently. Jack raises the axe against one that attacks him. He throws it against the wall and swings the axe at its head, removing the top just above the ear. The zombie drops like a rag doll. Beth dodges the zombie coming for her and as if doing a martial arts move reverse punches the zombie followed by the business end of the wrench coming down on its head. It drops. Jack addresses the third zombie. He brings the axe down on its chest, embedding it there. The weight of the axe drops the zombie to its knees and Beth grabs a screw driver from the control panel and inserts it into the zombie's left eye. The zombie drops motionless. Jack closes the Control Room door.

Jack quickly opens the small arms locker and snags a pair of Glock 22s and four clips. He hands one of the weapons to Beth and a pair of clips. Beth pops a clip into the gun, chambers a round and sets the safety. Jack smiles at her. She shrugs and tries to force back a return smile.

Jack turns his attention to the console. He searches the console and finds a large red button enclosed in a glass case. "The key is on his ring," Beth instructs. Jack sifts through the keys on Cliff's ring and finds a small key that fits the lock. It pops open. A computer screen awakens in front of them with "Self Destruct Sequence" instructions. Jack types on the keyboard to enable the sequence. "Zero, zero, zero, zero," Beth advises, sharing the self destruct password with Jack. Jack looks up at her. "He wanted something easy to remember," she quips. Jack types it in.

"Self Destruct Enabled. Press red button on the console to begin 5 minute countdown. Evacuate all personnel immediately" appears on the screen. The timer above the red button sets to 5:00. "You ready?" Jack asks. Beth stares at Jack for a long second as a tear forms in her eye. The thoughts of her dead mother, father in danger and the institute which had been her whole life now being destroyed overwhelm her. Jack takes her hand and gently kisses her. She squeezes his hand. Beth reaches down and presses the button. "Self destruct sequence activated.

You have five minutes to evacuate",a computer voice drones over loudspeakers.

CHAPTER 23

Jack and Beth unlock the service entrance door at the rear of the control room with weapons drawn. Panting lightly as if playing a tense video game, they look up and down and discover movement in both directions. The door clicks closed behind them, drawing the attention of both groups of undead. The top group reaches first, where Beth is. She fires the Glock and dispatches one, then another, then another. Jack fires on the group approaching him from below. Heads splatter the wall with slimy brain matter and coagulated blood. The shots create a deafening noise. A nurse zombie charges Beth, slamming her into the wall. Beth grunts and struggles. The female undead snaps her jaw at Beth. Beth struggles to keep her defense up. Another zombie falling over knocks Beth's arm away, giving a clean lane to Beth's face to the zombie. Beth screams. Jack lunges in and pops the second invader in the temple and grabs the female zombie. They struggle and Jack lifts her up and tosses her like a rag doll over the stair railing, plummeting her to the floor below, where the hand rail decapitates her. Beth collects herself.

They change clips and head downstairs. "You now have four minutes to evacuate",drones the speakers on each floor. Beth and Jack pick up the pace. Another group of zombies charge from below. Eight pops of gun fire leave a heaving pile of already dead corpses in their wake. They reach the bottom and carefully open the exit door to the garage.

They enter the garage and are met by four more zombies. Beth empties her clip eliminating the two on her side. Jack head shots the two on his side in rapid succession. The random thought hits him that he's getting pretty good at this. He's not sure if that should be considered a positive or a negative. "I'm out," Beth declares. Jack checks his clip.

"Two rounds left. Let's find the car," he responds.

The door behind them swings open. Jack and Beth whip around, Jack with weapon already cocked. Cliff barges through the doorway. "Daddy!" Beth exclaims and runs to him. They embrace tightly. Jack smiles. A zombie sneaks through the door behind Cliff. Jack's eyes widen. Cliff and Beth are oblivious to the zombie just being happy to be reunited.

"Cliff!" Jack yells. Beth opens her eyes and screams. Cliff, not seeing the zombie but knowing he can't save them both, shoves Beth as hard as he can, launching her back to Jack. He turns to face the zombie who is already on him. They wrestle. Jack tries to target the zombie with his Glock but can't get a good shot. The zombie leans on Cliff, bending his knee sideways. Cliff shrieks. He finally gets leverage and pins the zombie to the wall. Jack races up and puts his second to last shell in the zombie's eye. It drops.

"You now have three minutes to evacuate",the computer voice drones. Cliff strains to stand and bends over to catch his breath after that. Jack glances down to see blood running down Cliff's sleeve from the inside. "Cliff?" Jack asks, already knowing the answer before the question will escape his lips. Cliff looks down at his arm. He raises his sleeve. Bite marks. Beth looks at the wound and tears roll up in her eyes.

"Fuck," Cliff exhales.

"Let's go. We can treat you when the CDC gets here," Jack replies. Cliff looks at Jack and then at Beth. He smiles.

"You saw the data Jack. I can already feel the change. We don't have time. And I certainly can't run on this knee," Cliff surrenders.

"Daddy, please," Beth pleads. Cliff smiles at Beth and touches her cheek.

"It'll be alright. I'm going to be with your mother," Cliff whispers.

"Daddy, no," Beth sobs.

"Come on Cliff, we have to try. We'll help you. If we hurry…" Jack negotiates.

"You now have two minutes to evacuate." The computer rudely interrupts.

"You know what to do," Cliff tells Jack. Jack's eyes swell with tears.

"I can't," Jack replies with a breaking voice.

Cliff stares at Jack for a long minute. "It's been the pleasure of my life to work with you Jack. You're like a son to me. I see so much of myself in you. You can fix all of this. The two of you. It's up to you now. But be careful who you trust. Not everything is as it seems," Cliff says. The sound of movement comes from around the corner. Beth holds Cliff. Cliff kisses her head. "Don't let me suffer Jack. I beg you. You can do this. You have to do this."

Cliff bends over in pain. He drops to his knees. Jack draws his weapon. Beth sobs. "Take care of my baby girl, Jack," Cliff implores. Jack nods yes through tears. Cliff's breathing shallows. He raises his chin to improve his air way. Jack points the gun at Cliff's forehead. Cliff's eyes gloss over. Zombie Cliff leans forward toward Jack. Jack fires the gun. Cliff drops. Jack screams. Beth holds him.

Movement to their left interrupts the moment. Jack grabs the keys and chirps the car. Fifty yards to the right. Jack and Beth take off toward the sound. A zombie attacks. Jack shrieks in rage and clothes lines the zombie to the deck. They reach the vehicle. Two more zombies approach from behind the car. Beth dodges the zombie and kicks it in the back as she gets in the car. On the driver's side, Jack pounds the zombie's head into the window, smashing both.

"You now have one minute to evacuate", the computer warns. Jack starts the car and slams it in reverse. He looks behind him to find another zombie. He hits the gas and rams the zombie, launching it ten feet into a pillar. An arm comes off and it gets disemboweled. Two more zombies pound the hood. Jack shifts into drive and hits the gas. The zombies collapse and are run over by the car, crushing them. Blood and organs squirt in all directions. More zombies line the drive path. "You now have thirty seconds to evacuate." The computer delivers a final warning.

Jack weaves through more zombies. Zombies fly to the left and right. A security chain door blocks the exit. "Gun it," Beth commands. Jack floors the gas pedal. They hit the security door doing forty miles per hour and the door explodes open in a loud bang as the hinges break. Somehow the SUV made it through the barrier. Jack sighs heavily and looks at Beth. Beth looks at Jack in bewilderment.

They race down the hill to the street. Jack keeps the pedal floored as they screech into the left hand turn at the bottom of the hill. Back in the institute, the computer counts down. Five. Zombies wander the halls, seeking new sources of blood and tissue to feed on. Four. Zombies creep through the now open parking garage. Three. Zombies feed on corpses. Two. Zombie Cliff lays motionless. One. Zombie Rachel lies prostrate with the bullet hole between her eyes a somber reminder of her horrors.

The building explodes. Gigantic fireballs blast their way through the corridors, hallways, labs and parking garage. The intense heat vaporizes every zombie it touches. Each undead person is set free from their endless torment by the all consuming fire. When the fireball recedes, numerous fires remain. But there are no zombies. The tragic loss of life is enormous, and it's not lost on Jack. Nor is the responsibility that now falls on his shoulders. This may have been the end of this battle, but it's only the beginning of the war against the ZnMBe.

CHAPTER 24

Jack stops the car and looks back. Beth turns to survey the damage. The institute looks like a war zone. A random zombie is on fire and drops to the ground. Jack and Beth look at each other. Jack drives on.

They approach the road block Dr. Norris set up earlier. Several black SUVs and police cars block the path ahead. Jack stops the car. Several police officers point their weapons at Jack and Beth's SUV. "Raise your hands and step out of the car slowly," commands an officer. Jack and Beth raise their hands and slowly open the doors. They pour themselves out of the front seat with hands raised.

"Who are you?" the officer asks.

"Jackson Hart and Beth Barrister," Jack offers. Dr. Norris approaches them.

"It's alright officer. They're cleared," he instructs. The officers lower their weapons. Jack and Beth lower their hands and walk to Dr. Norris. "My name is Dr. Norris. Cliff emailed me a few hours ago about a possible outbreak. Where is he?" Dr. Norris summarizes. Jack looks somberly at Beth, not wanting to make her relive the tragedy.

"Cliff and Rachel didn't make it. Nobody did but us," Jack reflects. Dr. Norris looks suspiciously at Jack. He tries to figure out if Logan could have made it out without their knowledge, or worse if these two were capable of something sinister. The truth eludes him.

"Nobody?" Dr. Norris asks again. Jack shakes his head no. "What of the compound?" Dr. Norris inquires.

"Contained using self-destruct," Jack declares. Dr. Norris studies Jack for a moment and nods his acceptable response.

"We were very close to reversing the effects of the compound. I have the research, we just need time," Jack advises. This gets Dr. Norris' attention.

"You have the files?" he asks.

"Yes," Jack replies.

"Good. Let's get it back to the CDC. Is it in your bag?" Dr. Norris follows up. Something about the way Dr. Norris asks the question leaves a bad taste in Jack's mouth. He suddenly remembers the warning Cliff gave him about not everything being as it seems and a chill runs down Jack's spine.

"Nobody knows as much as I do about this compound," Jack declares, sending a subtle message of his trust issues.

"Good. You can consult. We have the best minds in the world waiting to get started on this," Dr. Norris advises. By the best minds, he's of course talking scientists at the Department of Defense. Jack begins to realize what is really going on here. But what can he do about it? Dr. Norris holds out his hand. Jack slowly opens his bag. He retrieves a flash drive and stares at it for a moment. He must think fast if he is to stay a step ahead of this. He hands it to Dr. Norris. "Excellent. Let's get you two debriefed. Go with these gentlemen," Dr. Norris instructs.

Two agents in black suits escort Jack and Beth to a waiting van. They open the door and Jack and Beth enter and sit. One of the agents closes the door. "What?" Beth asks Jack, seeing the obvious concern in his face.

"Something is wrong," Jack whispers. Beth looks wide eyed at him as if to ask what. "Your dad warned me about this. That not everything is as it seems," Jack continues.

"And you just gave them the flash drive?" Beth exclaims. Jack looks around and reaches into his front pocket. He shows the flash drive with the Hicks logo to Beth.

"Nope. I gave them my research into the compound. But it won't take them long to figure that out. But I have a plan," Jack explains. Beth looks around nervously.

Dr. Norris enters a van. He pulls a laptop out of a bag and plugs the flash drive into it. A file directory for ZnMBe loads. He opens a chat window on his laptop and types. "Logan failed. But I have the files. Cliff and Rachel Barrister dead. We have Beth Barrister and intern Jack Hart. All indications new biological weapon with definitive military applications successfully tested positive. Institute containment successful. No other witnesses. Bringing Jack and Beth in for debriefing. Report to SECDEF will follow up when scope identified. Will feed a cover story to the press and CDC. Be back at HQ in the AM. Uploading files. Norris out." He launches a Defense Department application and copies the files. He smiles.

A driver enters the van where Jack and Beth sit. He wears a black suit and aviator sunglasses. Noise coming from his ear piece gets his attention. He glances back at Jack and Beth, starts the van and drives.

A mile away from the institute, in a field, lies a large sewage drain pipe. Normally it's quiet as critters and insects come and go. The occasional drainage from rains the previous night release here. But today, a different kind of waste approaches the mouth. Several zombie rats scurry out of the opening. A zombie homeless man peeks into the sunlight. His glossed over eyes stare straight ahead. A residential neighborhood peeks over the top of the next hill. The rats scurry in every direction. The zombie homeless man heads toward the sights and sounds of the residential neighborhood, where he used to live.

THE END

CHECK OUT OTHER GREAT ZOMBIE NOVELS

RUN
by Rich Restucci

The dead have risen, and they are hungry.

Slow and plodding, they are Legion. The undead hunt the living. Stop and they will catch you. Hide and they will find you. If you have a heartbeat you do the only thing you can: You run.

Survivors escape to an island stronghold: A cop and his daughter, a computer nerd, a garbage man with a piece of rebar, and an escapee from a mental hospital with a life-saving secret. After reaching Alcatraz, the ever expanding group of survivors realize that the infected are not the only threat.

Caught between the viciousness of the undead, and the heartlessness of the living, what choice is there? Run.

THE DEAD WALK THE EARTH
by Luke Duffy

As the flames of war threaten to engulf the globe, a new threat emerges.

A 'deadly flu', the like of which no one has ever seen or imagined, relentlessly spreads, gripping the world by the throat and slowly squeezing the life from humanity.

Eight soldiers, accustomed to operating below the radar, carrying out the dirty work of a modern democracy, become trapped within the carnage of a new and terrifying world.

Deniable and completely expendable. That is how their government considers them, and as the dead begin to walk, Stan and his men must fight to survive.

CHECK OUT OTHER GREAT ZOMBIE NOVELS

Z BURBIA
by Jake Bible

Whispering Pines is a classic, quiet, private American subdivision on the edge of Asheville, NC, set in the pristine Blue Ridge Mountains. Which is good since the zombie apocalypse has come to Western North Carolina and really put suburban living to the test!

Surrounded by a sea of the undead, the residents of Whispering Pines have adapted their bucolic life of block parties to scavenging parties, common area groundskeeping to immediate area warfare, neighborhood beautification to neighborhood fortification.

But, even in the best of times, suburban living has its ups and downs what with nosy neighbors, a strict Home Owners' Association, and a property management company that believes the words "strict interpretation" are holy words when applied to the HOA covenants. Now with the zombie apocalypse upon them even those innocuous, daily irritations quickly become dramatic struggles for personal identity, family security, and straight up survival.

ZOMBIE RULES
by David Achord

Zach Gunderson's life sucked and then the zombie apocalypse began.

Rick, an aging Vietnam veteran, alcoholic, and prepper, convinces Zach that the apocalypse is on the horizon. The two of them take refuge at a remote farm. As the zombie plague rages, they face a terrifying fight for survival.

They soon learn however that the walking dead are not the only monsters.

www.ingramcontent.com/pod-product-compliance
Lightning Source LLC
Chambersburg PA
CBHW052001170626
46808CB00007B/2715